DECEIVED

Jennifer Sights

ISBN-10: 0-9890838-9-6
ISBN-13: 978-0-9890838-9-8

Author Info:

Website: www.JenniferSights.com
Facebook: http://www.facebook.com/jennifersightswrites
Email: jsights@gmail.com
Twitter: http://twitter.com/JenniferSights

ACKNOWLEDGEMENTS

I want to thank everyone who has been so patient waiting for this book. It's been a long road with more than a few craters along the way, but we made it!

Thank you to Chase Night for his fantastic story consultation and Jason Whited for being the most awesome editor ever!

Thanks to Denise Wy for the gorgeous cover design. www.coveratelier.com

Cover photo by chaoss / www.shutterstock.com

Thanks to Casey Carrington of Chalk & Soot for author photograph. www.chalkandsoot.com/index.html

To my best friend, who helped me find the story I didn't even know I was writing.

CHAPTER ONE

"You've come a very long way to hire me, Mr. Scope," I said to the middle-aged man sitting on the other side of my desk. Bloodshot eyes suggested he was a heavy drinker, or hadn't been sleeping well, or both.

"As I explained on the phone, I think my wife is involved with that guy I saw on trial, Jonah Carter, so I thought you'd be the best choice to help me catch her in the act." He sat slouched slightly, leaning forward in the chair.

Wesley Scope had driven to Saint Louis all the way from Memphis. I normally wouldn't consider cases from such a long distance–least of all because of private investigator licensing requirements–but when I heard the name Jonah, I couldn't say no.

"Are you certain it was him?"

"Ms. Ronen, do you think I'd have driven five hours on a whim? Of course I'm certain." His face turned red and a vein throbbed in his forehead.

"Please, calm down. It's just that I must be absolutely certain you aren't mistaken. I'll have to work with the City of Memphis to get approval to investigate since I'm not licensed in the state. And I rarely take cases outside of the Saint Louis area." I leaned back in my chair.

He took a deep breath then let it out. "I'm sorry, Ms. Ronen. I'm very upset that my wife seems to be gambling our life savings away, and then I see her with this criminal. I'm certain it's the guy I saw on TV during the trial of those witches. You have to help me."

I fought to keep my face neutral at his tone when he said, "those witches." "What exactly do you want me to help you with, Mr. Scope?"

"I'd like you to find out how my wife is spending all our money, and why she's spending time with that man. Is she cheating on me?"

I could tell I was going to have to work for every bit of information. "Why do you think she's gambling?"

"Could I have a drink of water?"

"Of course." If that's what it took to calm him down, it was no trouble to me. Vittorio had finally convinced me to move into a nicer office in Clayton, a much better part of town than where I'd worked when I met him. It even had a water cooler for occasions such as this. I got a glass from the rack next to the cooler and filled it for him. I refused to use plastic cups, hating the waste they created. Same for those little single-serving coffee pods.

Mr. Scope took a long drink before continuing. "Katie has a gambling addiction. She started going to meetings for it a few years ago, and it seemed like she had stopped. But now there are large sums of money withdrawn from our bank account, and I have no idea what she's spending it on. She's been very sneaky lately."

"Sneaky in what way?"

"She's secretive with her phone. Gets defensive if I walk in the room while she's checking email on her computer. Doesn't tell me where she's going a lot of the time…" he trailed off.

"Is she still going to her meetings?"

"I think so. I've followed her a few times, and she at least goes into the building. But I always see her leave with Jonah, and it's still several hours before she comes home after that."

In any other situation, I'd have been inclined to believe Mr. Scope's suspicions. But if Jonah really was involved, I knew there had to be something more sinister than gambling and a mere love affair going on. And I knew it would be in my—and all stregas'—best interest to find out what. "Though it is highly unusual, I will take your case, with one stipulation. If it turns out that Jonah is not involved, I will ask that you find a local PI to further assist you. Agreed?"

"Yeah, okay. Thanks." He reached across the table and shook my hand with a good, firm handshake.

After getting all the information I needed from Mr. Scope about the case, I walked him to the door. Unease filled my mind over the prospect that Jonah might be involved in something nefarious down in Memphis. I knew he'd moved there with the permission of his parole officer, and that Michael had gone with him after being asked to leave the Saint Louis coven. Michael had been sharing information with Samuel, who was still in prison, and I knew we couldn't trust him.

I wanted to discuss this with Vittorio, but he was in a business meeting all day. He had stepped down as CEO of Porter Enterprises, but only to a senior vice president position. He was less busy than before, but still had more meetings and business trips than either of us would like. Having Power made his position at the company tenuous, as public outrage and discrimination against stregas grew, and the board questioned the wisdom of keeping one of the most visible stregas in the country employed with them. He certainly couldn't afford to step out of a meeting with a potentially large client to talk to his girlfriend right now. But a delay could prove dangerous, so I would have to ignore my discomfort and start making plans for the trip to Memphis.

CHAPTER TWO

The next day I had a video call with the leaders of the Memphis coven. It was etiquette to let coven leaders know if you were going to visit their city. I also wanted to find out if they knew anything about what might be going on with Jonah, and explained what little I knew.

Rozanne and Jim Maryn sat far enough back from the webcam to share the screen. Rozanne's long scarlet hair made her blue eyes sparkle even brighter. I hadn't met them yet and could only imagine how vivid she would look in person. Jim, while attractive, seemed ordinary next to her with his mousey brown hair and hazel eyes.

I felt very alone without Vittorio by my side, but he had more business meetings he couldn't get out of, and after telling him about the case the previous night, he agreed it shouldn't wait.

"I'm sorry, we don't know anything that Jonah has been doing. He asked to join our coven when he moved here, but we denied him because of his past. We did let Michael join, however," Rozanne told me.

That was news to me. "Why did you do that? He was giving Samuel information in prison."

"That wasn't a good enough reason in our minds. Everyone makes mistakes." Rozanne raised an eyebrow, and I knew she was referring to Vittorio's previous infidelity. "Sometimes those mistakes must be forgiven."

4

I sighed, knowing I couldn't argue with her on that point. "Have you noticed anything strange going on in your community lately?"

The Memphis leaders shared a look. "There have been a few people who approached us about joining the coven. Once we determined that they truly had Power and were ready to accept them, they decided against joining," Jim said.

It was my turn to raise my eyebrows. "Did they say why?"

"No. They all just said they changed their minds. No one gave much of a reason, and we don't know what they've done in place of joining our coven. We've tried to find out, but frankly, it isn't high on our priority list. We're still dealing with a lot of media backlash, not to mention there are dozens of people who have no real Power that want to join, wasting our time. There are some real crazies out there," Rozanne said.

"Can you give me the names and contact information of those who didn't join? It might help if I can interview some of them. I know it's not related to my case, but if Jonah is involved, I think I should check this out too."

"Normally I would say no to protect people's privacy, but given the circumstances, I'll give you a few of the names," Rozanne said.

"Thank you. Do you know Wesley or Katie Scope?" I held a picture of Katie up to my webcam.

After a pause, they shook their heads. "No, I've never seen her," Rozanne said. "Let me check our records just in case." She seemed to click through some files on the computer, then returned her attention to me. "No, she's never approached us."

"I'd hoped you'd be able to give me more to go on. I'll find what I'm looking for either way, but I'd like to find it sooner rather than later if Jonah is involved."

Rozanne and Jim gave me some hotel suggestions and told me some places the coven members frequented to help me get started. I thanked them and then ended the video conference.

The next day I was on my way to Memphis. Vittorio wouldn't be able to join me for a few days, so I had plenty of time to think on the drive down. I couldn't imagine what Jonah would be doing, but it was all too coincidental that Mr. Scope saw his wife with him, and that some potential members of the Memphis coven had decided not to join. Most covens had more wannabe witches pounding on their door than they could handle; no one would turn down an opportunity to join without a very good reason. I'd spent much of the night before running background checks on the names Rozanne had given me, and my brain was working overtime trying to make connections.

After I checked into the hotel, I met Rozanne and Jim for a late lunch. I hadn't wanted to accept, instead preferring to get to work immediately, but Vittorio told me it was more required etiquette for a visiting strega. We made small talk, which I hated, before talking about the reason I was there. On the surface, it seemed that those who had decided against joining their coven had nothing to link them together, which didn't make my investigation any easier.

After lunch, Rozanne and Jim insisted on showing me where their coven held ceremonies. They drove me to a large cabin in the woods, more than an hour west of Memphis, near Village Creek State Park.

Inside, the cabin proved to be very nicely decorated, with a fully stocked kitchen and one full bathroom. "Members of our coven will sometimes come here for a night or two when they need to get away and reconnect with Goddess," Rozanne said by way of explanation.

"Who owns the cabin?"

"We do," Jim replied.

"That's very generous of you," I said.

"It was Rozanne's idea," Jim beamed, his love for her clear.

"We understand how hectic our world is, and the disconnect it can cause in our lives. Not all of our members are able to afford to get away on their own, so we like to be able to help them with that," Rozanne said.

Vittorio was more than able to afford a cabin somewhere off the beaten path. I'd have to talk to him about this idea later.

They showed me around the kitchen then took me for a short walk on the trail leading into the woods. As we walked, I suddenly felt as if someone was watching me. I turned and scanned the trees.

"Is everything okay, Elena?" Rozanne asked.

"I thought I heard something,"

She chuckled. "There's a lot of wildlife around here. You'll always hear a lot of movement in the trees."

I'd spent plenty of days birdwatching with Vittorio and felt defensive at her tone. "I realize that, but I felt like I was being watched. I know what deer sound like in the woods. This was different, larger." I listened for a few more moments but did not hear the noise again. Gradually, the feeling of being watched left. "It's gone now, anyway."

"It could have been a bear. You should be careful if you're ever out here alone. There have been a few sightings. Though I have managed to come to a sort of agreement with them," she said.

Now it was my turn to laugh. "An agreement? With bears?"

She did not blink. "Yes. I am quite fond of animals and have had an affinity for them since I was a child. It turns out that communicating with them is one of my Powers."

That was a new one to me. Though I could see how it could be extremely useful.

"I do not use my Power for anything other than keeping my coven safe from the wildlife out here...and having the occasional conversation with animals," she smiled.

"The trail is quite long and weaves through the entire forest. We'll turn around now and head back," Jim said.

"This is a wonderful place you have. It's very peaceful," I said. "I really would like to get back to town, though, so I can start working on the case."

"Of course," Jim said.

"I don't mean to be rude, but if Jonah is involved, I don't want to delay any longer."

CHAPTER THREE

It was nearly seven o'clock when I finally got back to the hotel. Katie Scope's Gamblers Anonymous meeting was starting at 7:30. I changed into jeans and a solid-colored T-shirt so I'd be less conspicuous and then headed to the meeting location. I didn't plan to go inside but wanted to watch for Katie to leave at the end to see where she went, and with whom.

At 8:45, she came outside. She looked to be in her late thirties and battling metabolism, but mostly winning.

Right behind her was Jonah. I could never forget his face and my Power recognized him immediately. I strengthened my shields without even thinking, both because I didn't want him to sense me and in reflex from the past horrors suffered at his hand.

I shook my head to rid myself of those thoughts. Jonah had opened the passenger-side door for Katie. Once he was in, I started my engine. They drove west out of the city limits of Memphis, and I saw a sign for Fayette County. I followed them to a neighborhood of large, expensive homes and stopped more than a block behind them when they parked. A few minutes after I watched them walk inside a house, I continued past, thankful the address was clearly visible.

I wondered whose house it was. Jonah hadn't been wealthy back in Saint Louis, and it seemed unlikely that he had suddenly come into such great money. They were likely visiting someone; but whom?

As soon as I got back to the hotel, I searched for the Fayette County Assessor's website to look up the address. I found it easily, but the house was owned by Bauer Leasing.

A quick search for the company's website showed it was a small leasing company that owned its own property, unlike most property management companies. I found the owner's name and office information but knew it wouldn't do me much good. They wouldn't just tell me who was leasing the house. I'd have to figure out another way to solve that mystery.

CHAPTER FOUR

The next day I decided to call Mika Svorek, one of the people who had decided against joining the Memphis coven, to see if I could find out why. Mika was twenty-two years old and in her second year of college. A little digging told me she had taken a few years off to travel, was now studying music, and was the lead singer and guitarist of a moderately successful local band. Social media had plenty of pictures of her and her band. Mika had long, dirty blonde hair and ice-blue eyes. A piercing in her left eyebrow and snakebite piercings in her lip provided contrast to the delicateness of her face.

I didn't know Mika's schedule and was happy when she answered the phone on the second ring. "Hello, Mika. My name is Elena Ronen. I'm working with Rozanne and Jim Maryn. Do you have a few minutes?" I decided to leave out that I was a private investigator and not to mention Wesley or Katie yet, since I really had no proof that people deciding not to join the coven were related to my case.

"I was just getting ready to leave for class, but I could meet you for coffee later if you want." Just like that, no questions asked.

"Sure, what time would be good for you?"

"How about 1:30? There's a coffee shop on campus. Do you need directions?"

"I'll find it, thanks. I have long black hair with red streaks. See you then." I hung up, surprised at how readily she'd agreed to meet with a total stranger. Though suggesting a coffee shop on campus was smart; there would be plenty of people there to give a sense of safety.

I recognized Mika from her social media photos when she walked into the coffee shop. She wore a sleeveless shirt that showed her right arm tattooed in a full sleeve death and black widow motif. Her makeup was almost imperceptible other than smoky black eyeliner. I stood. "Hi Mika, I'm Elena Ronen."

She held out her hand for a good, firm shake. I was impressed. Most college kids had the handshake of a limp noodle.

"Nice to meet you, Mika. Can I buy you some coffee?" I asked, wanting to put her at ease.

"That would be wonderful, thanks." She ordered an iced mocha, and I got a regular latte, then we sat down at a small table.

"So you said you're working with Rozanne and Jim? I hope they aren't upset I decided not to join their coven." Her brow furrowed.

"Not at all, they're just curious why. They're swamped, so I offered to help them. There have been a few other people who decided not to join, and they want to find out if there's something they could do differently so they can best help all stregas in the community."

"They didn't do anything wrong. I just found a coven that seems to fit my personality better," she said, sipping her mocha through a straw.

"Oh?" I asked, raising an eyebrow. I didn't know of any other covens in the area.

"Yeah, turns out there's another smaller coven here that's kind of new. One of my friends told me about it."

"Who are the Sacerdotessa and Sacerdote of this coven?" I asked.

"They're kind of secretive. They only want the best witches to join and are very selective in who they talk with. I'm not supposed to tell anyone their names until I've talked it over with them first," Mika said, shifting in her chair. "And they use High Priestess and Priest. They say it makes everything seem more accessible."

I took a sip of my latte. "Do you mind telling me how your friend knew about the coven?"

"Not at all. I told her how excited I was to be talking with Rozanne and Jim, that I'd finally be able to be with a group of people who really understood me and could help me refine my Power. She asked me if I'd want go with her to one of her coven's meetings. I didn't even know she had Power, or that there was another coven, but I was curious."

"What is your Power?" I asked.

She fidgeted as if the question made her uncomfortable. "I've always been good with animals, but felines especially. I almost feel like I can talk to them but not quite. When I was in grade school, I went on a camping trip with my family. I got lost in the woods. I remembered what they told me, to stay where I was so it would be easier for them to find me, so I sat under a large tree. As I waited, a cougar crept up to me. I didn't move a muscle, didn't even blink, but whispered, 'Please leave me alone, I mean you no harm. Please go away,' and it did!" She paused, pleased with the memory of her victory against nature. "I can also sometimes sense when someone else has Power as well, but I never knew what that feeling was until recently, since I never found anyone like me until–hey, you're the one who was involved in that trial, aren't you?" Her face lit up.

I was surprised it had taken her that long to figure out who I was. "Yes," I said.

"Well thank you. I know it was really ugly for you, but I'm so glad the world knows about magic now. I understand things about myself so much better, and I've found people who truly accept me."

I said nothing but wondered if she knew Jonah and recognized him from the trial as well. "So you can sense people's Power but didn't think your friend had any?" I prompted.

"Yeah. She doesn't. Not yet anyway. But the High Priestess says it's there, latent, and she just needs to be patient until her Power manifests."

I tried to keep my face neutral. As far as I knew there was no

12

way to tell if someone had latent Power. It was only discernible when the Power manifested, which could be at any age.

"You said this coven fits your personality better. Why is that?"

"There are a lot of younger people in it. But there are plenty of people older than me, too. They're all super open and casual at the meetings. The one I went to with Rozanne and Jim was so formal. I like the laid-back meetings and ceremonies better. I can ask if you can come sometime, if you'd like."

"That would be great," I said. I gave Mika a business card. "I really appreciate you being so open with me; it's going to help Rozanne and Jim a lot."

"No problem," Mika said, "Don't get me wrong, everyone at the meeting I went to seemed nice, but it just didn't fit my style. I'll let you know after I've talked to my High Priestess if you can come, and when." She stood, shook my hand again, and then walked out of the coffee shop after dropping her empty cup in the trash.

I remained at the table for a few more minutes, finishing my coffee and trying to process what Mika had told me. She seemed like a good person, though I sensed an undercurrent of danger to her. What I couldn't determine was, if it was danger to me, specifically, or just in general.

Back at the hotel, I called the other people Rozanne had given me contact information for. Most were not as open as Mika had been, though a few did give me a few minutes of their time. They all told me basically the same thing, that they preferred the more laid back and open atmosphere of this other coven, but they wouldn't tell me who the leaders were. I'd have to meet them to get a better feel for how they might be connected to my case, if they were at all.

Mika called me later that evening, just before I was about to go to sleep. "I asked if you could come to one of our meetings, but the High Priestess said no."

"Did she say why?" I asked.

"She said it was because you were leader of the Saint Louis coven and that there was no reason for you to be there because she knew you wouldn't join anyway."

That was odd. From what Vittorio told me, visiting stregas were always welcome at meetings and ceremonies in other cities. "Thanks, Mika, I appreciate you asking."

I called Vittorio to see if he had any ideas about what might be going on with this other coven. Unfortunately, he didn't but was just as suspicious of it as I was. "Be careful, *mio amore*, something is very wrong with this other coven."

"I will," I said, then lay down to sleep.

CHAPTER FIVE

The following night was the full moon, and I decided to take the day off from the investigation to reground myself. It had been a while since I had fully used the power of the full moon, and I wasn't sure where to go next with my investigation anyway. I spent the day in the woods at Rozanne and Jim's cabin, and would later meet the rest of their coven for the full-moon ceremony.

I was sad that I wouldn't be able to participate in the ceremony with my own coven–and Vittorio. I knew it would not be the same for them either, not having their Sacerdotessa present.

Rozanne introduced me to the coven as they arrived, including a girl who looked to be in her midtwenties. Bridget wanted to join the coven, and this was the first time she had attended any sort of ceremony. Excitement and nervousness radiated from her, and she kept pushing her short brown hair, which wouldn't stay tucked behind her ear, out of her eyes.

Michael was there as well. He stopped in his tracks when he saw me, eyes wide. It seemed he had not expected me to be there. I didn't know what to say to him and was relieved when he avoided me the entire night. I hadn't known him well in Saint Louis and didn't see any reason to make small talk with him now, either.

After the ceremony, I talked with Jim about what I had learned so far in my investigation. From the corner of my eye I saw Michael leaving with Bridget. "Do they know each other?" I asked.

"Not that I know of," Jim said.

15

Suspicious of why they would be together, I excused myself from the unfinished conversation and followed them.

Standing by a car, they spoke for a few moments. Then they got in separate cars, and Bridget followed Michael. I went to my car and started it after they had pulled away so they wouldn't hear the engine. Leaving the headlights off, I drove a safe distance behind them.

Once on the highway, it was easier to escape their notice. I followed them for over an hour until they finally stopped at the house I'd followed Jonah to the other day. First Katie Scope, now Bridget. Was Michael scouting potential stregas to lure away to this other coven? I wondered if Jonah had declared himself Sacerdote.

I parked several blocks away on a cross street to ensure I wouldn't be noticed. If they saw a car with Missouri plates, they'd surely be able to guess whose it was. The fact that it was a Mercedes SL500 didn't help in making it less obvious. I'd have to rent a car the next day to remedy this. I walked toward the house, hoping to be able to get close enough to see what was going on.

Hearing voices from the backyard, I snuck around, thankful for a full six-foot privacy fence to hide me from view. Peering through the slots in the fence, I saw a circle of people preparing for a ceremony. It seemed this was where the other coven met. I scanned the crowd, looking for any other familiar faces. Out of the twenty-five people there, I recognized Mika, then Katie, and of course Michael. He stood next to Jonah. A startled gasp almost escaped my mouth when I saw whom Jonah stood to the left of.

Shane. And to Shane's right was Evelynn. The former Columbia, Missouri coven leaders who had tried to take over our coven the previous year.

Last I'd known, they were in Florida, searching in vain for a coven to accept them. Vittorio and I had banished them from the Midwest, so the fact that they were in Memphis, and apparently working with Jonah and Michael, scared me. This could be disastrous.

"Mio amore, you realize that this means Evelynn and Shane know you are investigating them?"

"What do you...oh shit." That explains why Mika's Sacerdotessa said I wasn't welcome. Because her Sacerdotessa is Evelynn. That meant Shane, not Jonah, was Sacerdote. Double shit.

"You must be extremely careful everywhere you go. I will cancel all my meetings and be there tomorrow afternoon."

"You don't have to do that. I have my gun. I'll keep my shields up tight." I didn't want to interrupt Vittorio's business, but in truth I was relieved he would be with me sooner. To say I was scared would be an understatement.

"Your safety is my utmost concern, mio amore. I do not want to lose you."

There was so much emotion in his voice, I wondered if there was something he wasn't telling me. "What's wrong, Vittorio?"

I sensed him shaking whatever thought he'd had from his head. "I am simply worried about you. Evelynn and Shane are extremely dangerous."

"I know they are, my love, and I promise to be extra careful until you are by my side." Exhaustion made me sappy.

"Sleep, mio amore. I can sense you are tired. I will be with you tomorrow. *Ti amo.*"

"I love you, too," I said with a yawn and fell asleep with the phone still in my hand.

I dreamed of Kevin that night. It had been over six months since I had. In my dream, I relived his death, exactly as it occurred in real life. This time, though, I watched from outside my body. I stood next to Kevin, an invisible observer.

I watched myself translate the map for Clavius, watched him grow in Power. I knew what came next. My dream self stood between Elizabeth and Kevin, prepared to sacrifice myself instead. I tried to grab her wrist to stop her from plunging the knife into Kevin, but my hand passed right through. I screamed for Kevin to move, but he didn't hear me. I was truly invisible and silent, while the me who could be seen simply stood staring in horror.

17

This dream was worse than the reality had been because I knew what would happen and could do nothing to stop it. I watched him die, heard myself scream, saw the pain distorting my own face as I hadn't been able to see in reality.

When I finally forced myself awake, I sensed a presence in my hotel room. The light through the crack in the curtains was enough to prove no one was there.

I reached for my Smith & Wesson Model 10 and crept to the bathroom, the only place someone could be hiding. Nothing. I still felt as if someone—or something—was in the room with me. I turned on the lights, looking again, yet knowing I'd find nothing.

"Elenaaaaa," a voice whispered behind me. Kevin's voice.

I spun around, but of course he wasn't there. Kevin was dead, and it was my fault.

"Elena," the voice said again, louder this time.

"No, it's not real, stop, please," I said and fell to my knees. I dropped my gun and held my head, crying.

"Elena," it said into my ear.

"Stop!" I screamed, my Power rushing out from me, raw and wild. When it came back, the entity was gone, my hotel room silent.

Mio amore, what is wrong? Vittorio asked in my mind.

I was curled up, sobbing on the bathroom floor, barely able to tell him. I opened my shields just a little to let him see what I'd experienced.

I wish I was there to hold you, he said.

I've been doing so well, I said, picking myself up and wiping the tears from my face.

It may just be the stress from seeing Jonah again. I will come as soon as I am able. Please be careful, though I do not know if it is something to worry too much about. Jonah would bring back painful memories for you.

I splashed cold water on my face and blew my nose, then lay down in bed, Vittorio still in my mind. *Will you stay with me until I fall asleep again?* I asked.

Of course, mio amore.

Even without his physical embrace, I still fell asleep faster than

I'd thought possible.

CHAPTER SIX

My phone ringing woke me the next morning, though when I looked at the time I realized it was almost afternoon. I had been more exhausted than I thought. It was Rozanne, calling to tell me Bridget had decided not to join their coven. "Did you follow her when she left last night?" she asked as I yawned and wiped the sleep from my eyes.

"Yes. I was concerned by the fact that she was leaving with Michael and wanted to see if they went to the same place together." I told her what I'd discovered, while starting to brew coffee from the single-serving coffee maker in the room.

"That *is* alarming," Rozanne said.

"Yeah. Alarming is an understatement. But at least we know why people have been deciding against joining your coven. That's one mystery solved. Now I have to figure out what the hell they're doing here."

"You don't have to," Rozanne said. "Tell me the address of the house they're using and I'll go have a talk with them. They're encroaching on our territory and doing Goddess only knows what terrible things at their ceremonies."

The smell of fresh coffee perked me up a little. "I don't think that's a good idea, Rozanne. Evelynn and Shane are dangerous. They were dangerous before, and now that they haven't been able to find a coven to accept them, they're probably desperate. We need to approach this carefully. I'd like to wait until Vittorio gets here later today and discuss it with him. He's familiar with their Power."

"You have a point. When will he be here? I'd like to have you both over to discuss this at dinner."

I knew better than to argue about wasting precious investigation time with what promised to be a long, arduous dinner. After making arrangements, I hung up then set about tracking down anything I could about Evelynn and Shane online. Utility bills, bank accounts–anything I could access in an attempt to track where they'd been and what they might be doing. I finally confirmed that they were, in fact, the renters of the house in Fayette County.

The last place I could track them having lived was Pensacola, Florida. There was a three-month gap in any financial information I could find between that and their first payment on the house in Memphis. According to that first payment, they'd been in Memphis for three months. They'd been busy if they'd been able to recruit twenty people in that amount of time.

Now I knew where Wesley's wife was going after her Gamblers Anonymous meetings, but it still didn't explain what she was doing with their money.

I hated that Rozanne and Jim seemed to like talking so much more than doing, though I had to admit the meal Rozanne cooked was worthy of a five-star restaurant. Vittorio was able to convince them over lamp chops and a delicate rice pilaf to stay away from Evelynn and Shane, and to let us handle the situation, at least until we knew more about what was going on.

"We'd like to join the discussions about a central council," Jim said over dessert, which was a perfect lemon meringue pie.

I tried to keep my face neutral while Vittorio responded. They hadn't exactly been against the idea, but they refused to participate in any talks. Until now.

"What has changed your mind?" he asked.

"We don't like the fact that Evelynn and Shane are in town, when it was made clear to them that they were not welcome in the

Midwest, or that they may be luring stregas away from our coven. Perhaps if the edict had come from a stronger ruling body, they might have obeyed. We are willing to listen with open minds."

"That is wonderful to hear," Vittorio said. "The next meeting will be at the end of this month. I will send you the details."

"Thank you for keeping an open mind," I said.

After a cup of rich, French-press coffee, we were finally able to make our exit. "That was a colossal waste of time," I said when we were finally in Vittorio's Ferrari, headed back to the hotel. I'd felt captive to their idling discussions of the community and events that seemed trifling compared to what was going on right there in their own city.

"Mio amore, you know it was not. It is a big step that Rozanne and Jim are willing to join discussions of a central council."

"Yes, but they talk so much. Dinner could have been over in half the time. That's time I could have spent trying to figure out what Evelynn and Shane are up to. As it is, I'll have to wait till tomorrow, and I don't want to lose time."

"I understand, but do you not agree that it will be nice to have the rest of the night to ourselves?" Vittorio grinned.

"It has been a while since we got to just relax together. But you know my mind will be on the case, at least partly."

He sighed. "I know. And if I am honest, so will mine."

Kevin stood at the foot of my bed when I woke in the middle of the night. I did not move but gently nudged Vittorio. *Do not move, my love, but tell me if you see someone in the room*, I thought to him.

He turned his head slightly. *I see nothing, mio amore.*

Do you feel anything out of place? I really wanted him to sense something so I'd feel less crazy.

I do not. Nothing seems to be wrong. Are you all right?

I sat up in bed, but the figure did not move. "Why are you here?" I asked, unsurprised when I got no response.

Standing, I moved toward the figure. "Kevin?" Still no response. It just stood there.

When I reached out to touch his arm, my hand went right through the apparition, as if it were a ghost. But I didn't think it was a ghost. Not in the typical sense of the word, anyway. There would be no reason for Kevin's lost soul to be here in Memphis.

Unless he blamed me for his death. After many long months, Vittorio and my therapist had managed to convince me that he didn't, that it wasn't my fault. But if Kevin's ghost was here, maybe they were wrong and I was right.

The bed squeaked as Vittorio sat up and put his legs over the side of the bed next to where I stood. "Elena, there is nothing there," he said.

"Don't you see it? Kevin is right there, right next to me." My voice broke.

He stood and wrapped his arms around me. "Mio amore, you are imagining things. There is no one and nothing in this room except you and me."

The figure disappeared, so I let Vittorio pull me back into bed.

"I am beginning to worry about you," he said. "This case may be too much for you to handle right now."

"No! I can handle it. I have to find out what's going on. I won't feel safe until I do."

"But your sanity may not be safe if you continue investigating. You have worked hard in your therapy and have grown so much stronger. I do not want to see you lose any of your progress, or need to go back on medication."

I'd been off Zoloft for over nine months. My Power was much stronger and clearer without it. I didn't want to lose that control and clarity. "I know; I don't either. But I can't let this go."

Vittorio sighed. "You are so stubborn. But I will support you in every way I can. Just please let me go with you when you attempt to follow them?" He made it a question.

"Of course I will," I said, yawning, then snuggled back into his arms.

CHAPTER SEVEN

The next day I rented a car, ensuring it had Tennessee plates on it. I was even more on edge with the appearance of Kevin–or a specter that looked like him–and didn't want our Missouri plates or flashy cars to give us away.

Once we were safely in the nondescript Chevy Malibu, we headed to Fayette County, where we hoped to catch sight of Evelynn or Shane and follow them to wherever they might be going that day. It was a Monday, and I hoped most people would be away at their jobs and not home to notice an unfamiliar car parked on their street.

We sat in the car for two hours before the garage door opened and a Hyundai Genesis coupe pulled out. A woman was driving, and my gut clenched when I saw it was Evelynn. I took slow, controlled breaths to calm myself. She'd changed her hair–cut it short and dyed it mahogany–but my Power recognized her without a doubt.

I ensured my shields were firmly in place so she wouldn't sense me, and felt Vittorio do the same. His presence was no longer in my mind. Evelynn drove past the side street we were parked at the corner of, and when there was a safe distance I followed her.

"Elena, another car is pulling out of their driveway," Vittorio said when I'd only driven a block.

"Can you see who's in it?" I asked, continuing to drive.

"I cannot be certain at this distance, but it appears to be Jonah and Michael. They are coming this way."

"Well, nothing I can do without seeming suspicious. I'll just keep driving. Maybe you should slouch down a bit; you do kind of stand out," I suggested.

I giggled at the sight of tall, proper Vittorio trying to slouch in the little Malibu. It wouldn't help if they passed us but was the best we could manage. When we reached the end of the road, I turned the opposite direction as Evelynn, assuming Jonah would be following her.

Driving slowly, I was relieved to see in the rearview mirror that I was correct. Once Jonah turned the same direction as Evelynn, I found the nearest side street to turn around on, hoping I wouldn't lose them.

After catching up, but maintaining a safe distance, we followed them to downtown Memphis. Both cars pulled into a parking lot near a coffee shop. I continued past and parked on the next street over.

Vittorio stayed in the car. I put on a dark gray sweatshirt and pulled the hood up. It was so not my style, but I kept it with me for situations such as this to help disguise my looks a bit. I didn't stand out as much as Vittorio, with his six feet, four inches of height and long black hair, but my Gothic fashion sense still drew people's eyes in a crowd. Large sunglasses covered my eyebrow piercings and further hid my face. I wiped my blood-red lipstick off and replaced it with a delicate pink; a shade that made me cringe but further helped disguise my appearance.

I saw the three go into the coffee shop a block down the street. I crossed to the opposite side, ensured my shields were firmly in place, and then walked past, looking inside. They sat at a table with Bridget. I wished I knew what they were talking about, but that wasn't a Power I possessed.

I entered a sandwich shop and snagged a window table where I could watch for the group to leave then sent Vittorio a text letting him know what I was doing so he wouldn't worry. I ordered a sweet tea and half a turkey sandwich then sat down to wait, barely touching my food.

About a half hour later, Bridget walked out of the coffee shop in a hurry. She shook her head and seemed to be muttering to herself. I wondered what had happened.

A few minutes later the other three walked out. Evelynn turned to go back to her car, but Jonah and Michael walked my way. They'd be sure to see me at my window table, so I made a beeline for the back of the restaurant, throwing my trash away as an excuse. I made sure I was near the bathroom in case it looked like they would walk in, and sighed in relief when they didn't.

I had to make a quick decision; Evelynn would be long gone before I could go back to following her, so I decided to keep following Jonah and Michael. Again, I sent Vittorio a text to let him know the plan. I followed the two from a block behind until they reached an apartment complex. I made note of which building they went into and then headed back to the car.

When I got back to the car I told Vittorio what I'd seen. He didn't know what to make of it any more than I did. We decided to go back to the hotel and see what I could dig up on Bridget, and if it might give any insight into what happened.

Vittorio called Jim on the way back to see if he knew anything, but he didn't. He said he'd let us know if he heard from Bridget. He didn't like it any better than we did that she'd been talking with Jonah and Evelynn. "I still feel like they're just giving us the bare minimum to placate us," I said.

"They are extremely busy, mio amore, and it is better than not helping us at all," Vittorio said.

"I just wish they seemed to care more. This is their city. I thought they'd want to know about strange things going on, especially after hearing that Evelynn is in town."

I didn't find anything unusual about Bridget. Social media made getting to know someone's personality fairly easy–if they were honest, that is. The little bit I did know about her seemed to match her online persona. She'd been interested in witchcraft since she was a kid, and since news of our Power became public, she'd been blogging about her experiences with what she believed was her own Power. Nothing major had ever happened to her, but she had strange occurrences–like minor telekinesis and strong empathy– that she'd never been able to logically explain.

Empathy. I wondered if she sensed something off with Jonah and Evelynn, and if that's why she left so abruptly. I wished I could call her and ask, but then I'd have to admit to following the others. I decided to wait for now and see if she contacted us again.

I was surprised later that day when I got a phone call from Bridget. I hadn't given her my information and had only talked to her briefly the other night.

"Jim gave me your number," she said. "I hope you don't mind."

"Not at all, but can I ask why he told you to call me?"

"He said you were helping them figure out why potential coven members were turning them down in the end."

"I am. But that still doesn't explain why they'd ask you to call me." I didn't want her to know that I was aware of her conversations with the other coven's members.

"One of the members of the other coven, Jonah, approached me a week ago and said I might be more interested in their coven, so I decided to check it out, but something felt kind of off. I mean, Rozanne is amazing, she's so kind and has a great sense of humor. And everyone I talked to at the full-moon ceremony seemed friendly. But I wanted to check out all my options."

I debated asking her about Michael but decided to wait until I'd gained more of her trust. "How did they know to approach you?"

"Jonah sent me a message via my blog, so I guess that's it. We exchanged a few emails, and he said if I wanted to meet them that his best friend would be able to take me there the night of the full moon."

"Who's his best friend?"

"Michael. I don't know if you know him or not, but he's in Rozanne and Jim's coven."

"I've met him, though I don't really know him." True enough. "Would you mind meeting for coffee? I prefer face-to-face conversations whenever possible."

"Of course. I have to run a few errands this afternoon, but I'll be free around five. Maybe we could get drinks instead?"

I was able to tolerate a beer or two, so I agreed. Whatever would put her most at ease. She gave me the address of a bar downtown before hanging up, and then I filled Vittorio in. "I think I should go alone. I don't want to scare her off."

Vittorio was silent. "What if it is a ploy devised by Evelynn and Shane to harm you?"

"But how would they have known Jim would tell her to call me?"

"Maybe they were hopeful. I do not know, mio amore, but I do not like the idea of you going alone."

"I can take care of myself, and I'll have my gun."

"Yes, but remember what happened with Clavius? We were both overcome by his Power."

Clavius had managed to knock us both out in broad daylight. I would never forget that. "Of course I remember. But Clavius is not here, and I've battled Evelynn and Shane before. I can do this alone," I argued.

"What if I drive you but wait in the car so I will be close should you need me?" His brow furrowed.

Sensing he would not be happy until I agreed, I sighed and stopped arguing.

CHAPTER EIGHT

Vittorio dropped me off at The Flying Saucer at 4:45. I wanted to be sure Bridget wouldn't know I hadn't come alone. I needed to gain her trust so she'd be honest with me about what happened with the other coven, and I sensed she'd be intimidated by Vittorio. I claimed a booth toward the back of the bar and was sipping a stout when Bridget walked in. I stood and waved to her.

She waved back, ordered a mai tai, and then joined me.

Once we got the small talk out of the way, I guided her back to our conversation from the phone. "So Jim told you to call me?"

"Yeah, like I said, he told me you're helping them because they're so busy. But what exactly are you helping them with? I didn't quite understand."

"It seems as if they've had several people approach them about joining their coven, then change their minds at the last minute. They're curious why."

"Why would it matter?" Bridget asked.

"Usually, there's only one coven in a city, and they weren't aware of any other when they started losing potential members, so they wanted to know if they were doing something to turn people off."

"From what I've seen, they're more formal, so I can understand why some people would be more interested in the other coven."

"And you?"

She thought for a full minute before answering. "I did like that the other coven was more laid back. Their full-moon ceremony was more like a party, almost." She paused.

"But?"

"I met with them the next day. I was ready to join. But then they started talking about money. Like, there was a fee to join. When I asked them how much, they said it was flexible depending on what the member could afford. Rozanne and Jim hadn't said anything about fees, and that made me suspicious. But I kept talking to them, trying to find out more. They wanted to know how much I make each year and how much I'd be able to afford to donate to them each month. Something just seemed off, and I told them I had a lot of student loans and didn't make a lot and was barely making ends meet as it was." She glanced down at her drink. "It isn't true," she said sheepishly.

"That's okay; sometimes we have to stretch the truth to get to other truths," I said.

"Anyway, they kept pushing. They said I could pay in other ways."

"What other ways?" I asked when she didn't continue.

"I didn't stick around to find out, but I have some guesses. Look, I'm not stuck on myself, but I know I'm pretty. You can imagine where my mind went, and I want no part of that. So I left."

"As far as I know, you're the first one to turn Evelynn down," I said.

"I'd believe it. They're very persuasive, and some of the members…well, some of them don't seem to have any real Power, so they're probably desperate to be accepted. Especially the younger girls who are still finding themselves."

My stomach churned, and I knew I wouldn't finish the rest of my stout. I remembered what Shane had done to me. He'd mindfucked me and forced me to have sex with him. Evelynn would have killed Vittorio if I hadn't let Shane have my body. He and Evelynn were married, but it was a marriage of convenience. They had no qualms when it came to screwing other people. Especially if it furthered the needs of their coven, or their own desires.

"So you think they're tricking people with no Power into believing they might have some, so they'll join the coven?"

Bridget nodded, taking a long drink of her mai tai, and shuddering at whatever thought had just crossed her mind. "Why do you think they're asking for money? Is that normal?"

"No, it isn't," I said. "This isn't like a lot of mainstream churches that require tithing. We do this out of true belief and love for our fellow stregas. If we ever do need money, we might ask people to pitch in but do not require anything from any member. No matter what."

"So it was probably wise of me to tell them no." It wasn't a question, but I nodded anyway.

Bridget's eyes widened. "Wait a minute. From what you're saying, it sounds like they're not on the up and up. Like they're scamming people. If that's true, and if I'm the first person to turn them down, they're probably going to be afraid of what I might tell people outside their coven." She stared right into my eyes. "Am I in danger, Elena?"

She was smart, and I wasn't going to lie to her. "I don't know."

"Shit." She downed the rest of her drink.

"I can help keep you safe," I made my words a promise.

"How?"

"We can go talk to Rozanne and Jim right now. You can follow me," I said, forgetting I didn't have my car and that Vittorio was waiting for me. "I'm sure they'll let you stay with them for a while."

"So I'm just supposed to hide out until Goddess only knows when?" I sensed she was turning her fear into anger as a defense mechanism. It was a move I was all too familiar with.

"I'm not saying you have to hide. Only that you should be careful for a while. Stay in public; don't go places alone."

"Maybe I should have stayed to myself. Maybe I should have remained a solitary witch," she said, the anger already fading, her eyes shining with tears.

"Let me call my ride, then we'll talk to them and figure it out from there. It will be okay, I promise." I was not going to let another person die or get harmed on my watch. Not this time.

"Who's your ride?"

"My Sacerdote and boyfriend, Vittorio."

That made her smile. "You're lucky, you know that?" she said, sounding more like the carefree young woman she'd been when she walked into the bar.

"Life isn't easy just because you have a hot boyfriend," I said.

"It can't hurt though."

"No it doesn't," I laughed. I called Vittorio and gave him a brief rundown. "I don't like to drive if I've had anything to drink, so he went and had dinner after dropping me off." I'd been clean for six years, and was slowly easing my way back into social drinking. So far, I was managing just fine, but I didn't want to take any chances.

When we got to Rozanne and Jim's, I asked Bridget to tell them what she'd told me. They were outraged when she told them the part about money, and even more so over the mention of paying in other ways. They immediately agreed to let Bridget stay with them as long as necessary. They also said they'd arrange for other members of the coven to take turns being with her at all times.

"I don't need babysitting. I can take care of myself." Bridget crossed her arms.

"Bridget, what you may have seen of the trial on TV was awful, but you can't imagine what terrible things these people can do. You may think you understand, but believe me, experiencing it is on a whole other level. I'm still having nightmares because of it," I told her. "I know it's not going to be fun having someone with you all the time, but we'll do our best to make sure you still get your space and privacy." I paused and let all the pain of losing Kevin show on my face. "Please."

Her eyes widened when she looked at me. "All right, I'll trust you on this, but I don't like it."

"And please do not try to sneak away from your escorts at any time," Vittorio said, sensing that she might not be as compliant as we'd like. "The worst thing that could happen is for us to not know where you are should they attempt to harm you. They know that we are in town, and that we are investigating them. That knowledge will make them even more dangerous."

Bridget studied him for a moment. "I promise," she said solemnly.

"Thank you," I said, letting out the breath I'd been holding.

We excused ourselves so Rozanne and Jim could help Bridget get comfortable. They would take her to her apartment to get some clothes and personal items, as well as her books for school. She refused to miss any classes over this.

"That may have been the easiest case to solve I've ever had," I said once we were back at the hotel. The drive had been silent as we contemplated what we had learned and the task we faced. "I almost wish it had been much more difficult and hadn't led back to Evelynn and Shane. How could I have actually believed we might have seen the last of them?"

"It is all right, mio amore," Vittorio said, coming up behind me in the bathroom and wrapping his arms around me. "We have been faced with so many other problems, I had not given them any thought either. We have been remiss, and now we must fix that."

"Do you think any of the other coven members are in danger now?"

"I do not know, but it does not make sense that they would be. Bridget is the only one who has given us any useful information. I am worried about her safety, though. I wish she was not so headstrong."

"That stubbornness just might save her if things get ugly," I said, pulling on my black chiffon nightgown. I usually preferred to feel Vittorio's skin against mine while I slept, but I was edgy and feeling vulnerable because of the ghostly sightings in the hotel. The nightgown gave me a tiny bit of a sense of security that I knew was completely false; clothing would protect me from nothing, other than having some member of the press catching a nude photo of me. And nudity—my own, or anyone else's—didn't bother me.

"You know this will eventually leak to the media," I said as we climbed into bed.

"Yes, it will be more bad press for us to have to counteract." Vittorio paused and turned out the bedside light. "We will have to work closely with the local police. Tell them what we know so they can investigate and perhaps arrest them."

"That's a good idea," I said, yawning. The lack of sleep the past few nights was getting to me. "Tomorrow," I murmured, as I fell asleep on Vittorio's chest.

CHAPTER NINE

I again woke in the middle of the night to see Kevin's figure standing at the edge of the bed. It moved toward the door, and through it, into the hallway. I glanced at Vittorio, who slept soundly, and tightened my shields. I wanted to find out what this figure wanted, and knew if Vittorio woke he would try to stop me from following.

I got out of bed as quietly as I could then padded out into the hallway. The figure was at the end, by the door to the stairwell.

Closing the door behind me, I cringed at the click the latch made. Once in the stairwell, I caught the figure moving upstairs before I lost sight. I hurried after it, emerging on the hotel roof.

The figure stopped halfway to the edge and turned toward me. I had a clear look in the moonlight; it was indeed Kevin.

"What do you want?" I asked, but Kevin turned away and started moving toward the edge of the roof. "Wait!" I called after him then followed again.

Kevin stopped at the edge and turned to look at me. The look on his face beckoned me to follow, so I did. He stepped up onto the ledge by the time I reached him, and looked down. Then he turned his head, again beckoning me to follow.

"Kevin, don't do this, please," I sobbed.

He stepped back and fell from the roof.

"NO!" I screamed and reached for him, going over the edge myself in my desperate attempt to save him.

As he fell, he looked at me one last time, but the face was no longer Kevin's. His green eyes glowed with hellfire, his pointed teeth bared in a demonic grin. I screamed as I plummeted after him, realization dawning that I was chasing an image sent to harm me, destroy me even. And that it had succeeded.

Arms grabbed my waist, the air rushing out of me from the impact on my diaphragm. I continued to scream, but no longer felt like I was falling to my death.

Instead, I fell to the surface of the rooftop, its gravel biting into my skin. The nightgown did nothing to protect me from gravity. The delicate material was torn in several places, as were my arms and legs.

Vittorio cradled me close to his body while I regained my breath. "Mio amore, what are you doing?" Tears streamed down his face.

"I'm sorry, I'm so sorry. I don't want to leave you. I didn't mean to...I didn't know..." I trailed off, unable to form logical sentences through my sobs.

I had almost died, by what all but a few would consider suicide. I didn't want to die; not anymore. I had almost left Vittorio. Our bond was so strong, I didn't know how losing me in such a violent manner would affect him.

"Come, let me get you back inside. I will run a hot bath for you, and once you have calmed down you can tell me what happened. But for now, relax." He wrapped his arms tighter around me then stood, lifting me with him in one fluid motion. His strength and grace never ceased to amaze me. I nuzzled my face into his chest and wrapped my arms tightly around his shoulders and let him carry me back to the room as his scent calmed my nerves.

He cuddled me in the large Jacuzzi tub. I dozed as the hot water soothed me, safe in Vittorio's arms. When I had finally warmed up and calmed down, I told him what I had seen.

"It wasn't Kevin. It was...demonic," I finished.

"I do not think it was a demon, mio amore. I think it is someone trying to confuse your mind to deter you from continuing your investigation. It is likely Evelynn or Shane, though I cannot be certain."

"Do you think Chibuike could help us figure out who it is?" I asked. She had been a member of their coven in Columbia, Missouri, before we banished them from the Midwest, and was intimately familiar with their Power.

"She may be able to. I will call her as soon as we get you out of the tub and ask her to come immediately."

Chibuike had become one of my best friends. I still didn't form bonds easily and kept to myself outside of the coven. Sure, I still frequented The Chapel with Vittorio, but that wasn't the same as making true friends. The thought that Chibuike would be here to help reassured me. I did not doubt Vittorio, but I was terrified, and ready to call in the cavalry.

CHAPTER TEN

Chibuike arrived the following morning. I had barely slept the rest of the night, and was still shaken. Vittorio continued searching for information on the web while I sat in an armchair in the hotel room, nursing a cup of rapidly cooling coffee, staring at the floor.

When Chibuike walked into the room, I smiled almost imperceptibly. Setting the coffee cup down, I stood to greet her, and she hugged me tightly. Her brow furrowed when she pulled away.

"What is wrong?" Vittorio asked, seeing her expression.

"I feel something very...dark...connected to Elena. It feels familiar, but I'll need to probe deeper before I can be certain. Do you have anywhere to be this morning?"

"We cancelled everything for today so Elena could recover. What do you need to do?"

"I simply need to sit with Elena and have her open her mind to me, so I might be able to find what's causing her so much distress."

We sat cross-legged on the bed facing each other. I had opened my mind to Chibuike before, so the process was simple and familiar. I relaxed, counting my breaths, and let her search for whatever she had felt. After several minutes, she gently pulled back into herself.

"I felt you startle. What did you find?" I asked.

Vittorio sat next to me now, arm around my shoulders.

"It is Evelynn messing with your mind. I think I can break the connection, but it will leave you defenseless for a moment."

"How long of a moment?" Vittorio asked.

"No more than a second or two, but long enough for someone sinister to find their way in."

"Would it help if I shielded her with my own Power?"

Chibuike shook her head. "I can't hope to break the thread unless she is completely unguarded."

Vittorio tightened his arm around me.

I looked at him. *I can't keep experiencing this. I need her to break the connection.*

You know what you risk by doing this. He stared into my eyes.

I knew very well that I risked letting the blackness in again: the First Witch. "I almost died last night," I said aloud. "I'm willing to take the chance."

Vittorio didn't like it but couldn't argue. "Please, be fast," he pleaded with Chibuike.

"I'll be as fast as I am able, but there is no way to eliminate the risk entirely." She looked at me.

"Do it. Let's get it over with," I said, trying to sound braver than I felt. "What do I do?"

"Just relax and let me in as you did a moment ago. I need to find the root of the connection before I can break it. Once I do, I'll signal for you to completely drop your shields. I'll cut the thread, then you'll be able to raise your shields again."

"Will I feel anything?" My voice wavered.

"I don't think so but am not certain."

I let out a long breath. "Okay, let's do this." I shifted on the bed, getting as comfortable and relaxed as possible. Vittorio still had his arm around my shoulder.

"Vittorio, I'm sorry, but I need you to stop touching Elena during this. I fear if you do not, you will still be shielding her, intentional or not, and I won't be successful."

Vittorio took a slow, deep breath before removing his arm then went to sit on the desk chair across the hotel room from me.

"Ready?" Chibuike asked me.

I nodded. "Do it." Closing my eyes, I again concentrated on my breath and let Chibuike into my mind. She probed gently, like a soft spring breeze, brushing the corners of my mind. I knew she would be able to probe all my deepest, darkest secrets if she chose, yet I trusted her not to.

I felt an almost physical jolt as she bumped into something in my mind; something blocking her.

"I've found it," she said in a distant voice.

"Get rid of it," I pleaded.

"On the count of three, I need you to completely drop your shields." She emphasized "completely."

I nodded. "Okay."

She counted.

On three, I dropped my shields. The moment I did, I felt a snap, like a twig breaking, and knew the connection with Evelynn had been severed. I tried to put my shields back up, but the blackness engulfed me, crashing over me and through me like oily black waves. I fought to push it out but was helpless. I drowned in the blackness and knew the First Witch had found me.

Elena, a voice with a vaguely African, yet mostly alien, accent whispered in my mind, testing the feel of my name. *Elena*, it said again more confidently. *Is it truly you, my beloved? I have been searching for you for millennia. Finally, we will be reunited.*

I fought to raise my shields, to force the First Witch out of my mind, but could do nothing. I clutched my head, though all I felt was warmth and acceptance and beauty. I knew it was a lie; I knew the First Witch would make me his slave and inflict unimaginable tortures on me in an attempt to force me to do his bidding.

I fought as hard as I could, but knew I was doomed. The harder I fought, the more painful the encounter became.

I do not wish to cause you pain, heart of my heart. I beg you to stop fighting me.

That only made me fight harder.

The First Witch's sigh was audible in my head, and I felt the slightest of breezes from it. *I had hoped you would accept me into your life graciously. But I see now the depth of your spirit. I will enjoy breaking you. You will beg me to take you in the end.*

My world burst into a burning inferno hotter and brighter and more complete than any burning building I had ever seen. I knew I was lost, and rapidly losing the will to fight. *Yes, take me, just make the burning stop,* I thought groggily. My grasp on reality and consciousness was fading. All the fighting, all our work, had been for nothing. The First Witch now owned me.

CHAPTER ELEVEN

When I opened my eyes, I expected to find myself still in the awful inferno the First Witch had shown me. Was it hell? No, it was worse than hell. I would die before I gave in and let him take me.

Instead, I saw the hotel room. Vittorio cradled me in his lap on the bed, stroking my hair, his face tight with fear. I wrapped my arms around him, clinging to him as if he was my last chance at living.

"Mio amore. You have returned to me." He rocked me gently in his arms.

"The First Witch," I started.

"Sshhh," he murmured, holding me tight. "Rest. You were unconscious for almost an hour."

"How am I here?"

"Chibuike and I managed to join our Power to shield you and drive out whatever made its way into your mind. We feared it was too late."

I looked up at him, seeing how red his eyes were. Vittorio rarely cried, but I immediately recognized the signs. "I thought I was lost. I thought I was going to be torn away from you."

"Rest," Chibuike said softly.

"No, I have to tell you what happened. It's too dangerous to wait." I pushed myself up, and Vittorio propped some pillows against the headboard for me. "Is there any coffee?"

Vittorio chuckled. "You must not be too far gone if you are

asking for coffee."

I grinned weakly.

Chibuike rose to make me a cup of coffee from the little hotel room coffee maker. Thankfully, this hotel had passable coffee, though I'd have accepted even police station dregs at that point.

"Thanks," I said when she handed me the small Styrofoam cup. I cradled it in both my hands, still a bit shaky from my encounter with the First Witch, and no small amount of terrified.

I told them what happened, and how it felt like an eternity of pain and suffering.

"It was no more than five seconds," Vittorio said. "The moment Chibuike severed the connection to Evelynn, we knew something was wrong." He paused. "I do not know if I would have been able to save you alone. Even together, it was difficult."

Chibuike, much less formal than Vittorio always was, snorted. "Difficult is an understatement."

"I can still feel him," I said, starting to shake again.

Vittorio took the coffee from my hands, set it on the nightstand, and pulled me to him, soothing me with his Power until I stopped shaking.

"He's coming for me. He knows where I am."

"We'll do everything we can to protect you and help you fight him," Chibuike said. She sat on the edge of the king-sized bed.

"I fear it will not be enough," I said softly. "And we still have to find a way to stop Evelynn and Shane." A horrible thought crossed my mind. "What if they're working for the First Witch? What if they led him to me?"

"It is possible, I suppose, but I do not think it is likely. As far as I know, we are the only ones who are aware that he has awoken. I believe it is a coincidence, and that your shields being down let him find you. He must have been searching for you since he first felt you last year."

"I don't know which is worse—if they are working with him, or if they aren't," I said. "I guess it doesn't really matter. Either way, we have a huge battle coming our way." I paused. "Maybe I can beat him for good this time, and make up for my failure in my past life with him."

"Let us not think about that just yet. We will have to eventually, but for now we should focus on getting as much information as we can about Evelynn and Shane and their false coven, and about the First Witch. Chibuike, gather all the information you can about the First Witch. Elena and I will try to figure out what Evelynn and Shane are up to, and how we might stop them."

"It may be difficult; the only documents I've ever found are more legends and fairy tales than truth, but I'll contact some other stregas I know and see what I can find out."

"Thank you," Vittorio said. "What do you need right now, mio amore?"

"To sleep for a week solid. But that's not going to happen, so I guess we should get back to work. At least now I won't be trying to jump off any buildings in an attempt to save a demonic specter of Kevin." I sighed and felt Vittorio gently pushing at me with his Power.

"Elena, I cannot reach you. What is wrong?" His brow furrowed.

"I'm scared to let my shields down even a little. I'm afraid the First Witch will find me again. I don't know if I can survive another encounter." Another thought occurred to me. "How was Evelynn able to plant a connection in my mind? She knows that I'm here but hasn't seen me yet. Unless her Power has grown, she shouldn't have been able to do that without at least being in eyesight of me."

"I do not know, mio amore. I think we should ask Julian if he can come and help us. He may have some ideas as to how she accomplished this, and he might be able to help Chibuike find information about the First Witch, as well as help you strengthen and refine your shields."

"I'll take all the help I can get."

Julian said he would clear his calendar and be in Memphis the next day. Vittorio wanted me to spend the day resting, but I refused. "It's more important than ever to shut them down. I want to figure this out so maybe we won't have to worry about them at the same time we have to fight the First Witch."

Knowing I would not give in, Vittorio stopped arguing. My stubbornness–and Kevin's support–were the only reasons I was still alive today. Sometimes being stubborn got in my way, but more often it served me well. I agreed to go out to Rozanne and Jim's cabin with Julian the next day, which appeased Vittorio and Chibuike, though their tense faces gave away how fearful they were.

And who could blame them? Evelynn and Shane had proved to be more dangerous than we had suspected. That alone would be battle enough. But now that the First Witch had found me and invaded my mind, the stakes were infinitely higher.

"I have to call Wesley and tell him what we've discovered about his wife. I don't know how he'll take the news, but I'm sure it won't be well. Perhaps we can meet him for"–I looked at the clock, having no idea what time of day it was–"dinner. Will you go with me, Vittorio?"

"Of course, mio amore. I will not leave your side until this is over."

I didn't need my Power to tell me he feared that "over" would mean my death, or worse. I squeezed his hand.

Wesley demanded I tell him over the phone what I'd found, but I was insistent on delivering the news in person. I wanted to attempt to control his reaction.

I showered and dried my hair and put on the bare minimum of makeup. I didn't have energy for anything more. We met Wesley at Trolley Stop Market in downtown Memphis. The restaurant had a folksy vibe to it with shelves along the walls lined with goods from local farmers. I wished we had more time to browse, but Wesley was already there, a beer mostly empty.

I was famished after my encounter with the First Witch and ordered the largest entree I could find on the menu, along with a salad, and devoured the basket of sweet potato fries we got before dinner arrived. I opted for a Coke instead of beer or wine, afraid of anything relaxing my shields.

"What did you find?" Mr. Scope demanded the moment the waitress walked away with our orders.

"Your wife is not having an affair, nor is she gambling again."

"Then what the hell is she doing with our money?" He pounded the table with his fist.

"Has your wife talked about having Power?"

"Are you kidding? It's all she would talk about for weeks after that trial. She always thought there was something different about her, and that just confirmed it. I don't believe she really does have any Power, though. She talked about joining the local coven." He finished his beer as the waitress brought him another.

"What happened?"

"She talked about it every day but never did anything to get in contact with them. I wonder if deep down she knew she wouldn't pass their test?"

"And that was the end of it?" I prompted.

"Yes. Why? What is she doing?" He drained half of the fresh pint.

"She's joined a different coven," I said, watching his face.

"That's impossible! Why wouldn't she have told me?" He slammed his fist on the table again, shaking our drinks.

"Please, calm down, Mr. Scope," Vittorio said.

"Why should I calm down? My wife is doing God knows what behind my back, and you still haven't told me where my money is going." He drained the rest of his beer and signaled the waitress for another.

I wondered how many he'd had before we arrived.

"Mr. Scope," I began slowly, unsure how to best proceed. "We want to help you, but we need you to stay calm. I know this isn't a pretty situation. This coven that your wife joined...it isn't exactly sanctioned."

"What the hell do you mean 'sanctioned'?"

46

"The leaders are true witches, but they're not good people. No coven will accept them, so it seems they've gotten desperate and started their own, outside of all the rules we follow. They're recruiting both true witches and those with no Power. I believe they may be preying on members of various support groups. That seems to be where your wife met Jonah. And to make it even worse, they are requiring their members to make donations in as large amounts as they can afford. That's where your money is going."

"You have to be kidding me! This is ridiculous! I'm going straight to the media with this bullshit." He started to stand.

I reached across the table to gently grab his wrist. "Please, wait and hear us out."

We stared each other in the eye for a full thirty seconds before he sat back down.

"Thank you," I said then let Vittorio take over.

"If you go the media now, in this enraged and irrational state, imagine how it will look to the public. They may not differentiate between those who orchestrated this and those who were preyed upon. The public already greatly mistrusts us; if it comes out that some witches are misleading people, as well as extorting money from them, things will be even worse. You and your wife could face harassment. A very dear friend of ours has a terminally ill mother, who has no Power of her own, but because her son does, she has been harassed endlessly to the point where he cannot even safely visit her. Is that what you want for you and your family?"

"I want my wife–and my money–back; that's what I want," Mr. Scope said, a vein throbbing in his forehead.

"And we want to help you with that, but we need you to cooperate with us," I said. "Look, I don't do this, but I'm going to waive all my fees for this case. In helping you, we've uncovered a much larger problem that might have otherwise gone unnoticed for a long time. It will be easier to clean up the mess now than it would be months or years from now. I fully believe we can make this right, but we need you to be patient, and not go to the media."

"You're going to try to cover this up to protect your own," he accused.

Vittorio spoke. "On the contrary, Mr. Scope, we plan to go to the media ourselves soon to let the public know what is going on." He paused, and I sensed he was debating how much to say. "We think that if we break the story ourselves, are completely upfront and honest about it, that we might be able to minimize public backlash. We need to control this carefully to protect the innocent people who have been deceived."

I winced and rubbed my temples.

"Mio amore, are you all right?"

"Yeah, just got a shooting pain behind my eye. I'll be fine in a minute," I said, not sure that I would be. This was no ordinary headache pain. This was something different, though I didn't know what.

"Will you help us, Mr. Scope?" I asked, wanting to divert the subject of the unusual pain in my head back to the business at hand.

He sighed, picked up his beer, and took a long, slow drink before responding. "I guess so. What you say seems to make sense. But if you don't fix this soon, I will go to the media, don't you doubt that."

"I do not doubt it one bit, Mr. Scope," Vittorio said. "It is obvious how much pain this has caused you. I am truly sorry, and we will do everything we can to get your money back for you, as well as your wife."

"You better. Now if you don't mind, I'd like to drink the rest of my beer alone."

"Of course," Vittorio said.

"I'll let you know as soon as I have anything to share," I said. "I can't say how much we appreciate you helping us."

We both stood and shook Mr. Scope's hand before making our way to the bar.

"We would like to pay the bill for that table," Vittorio said, gesturing back to where Mr. Scope was sullenly finishing his beer.

We discovered that Mr. Scope had drunk quite a bit before we arrived.

"I'd also like to arrange for a cab to take that gentleman back home when he is finished drinking. I don't think it's safe for him to drive," I said, and Vittorio nodded his agreement.

CHAPTER TWELVE

I asked Vittorio to drive back to the hotel because the shooting pain in my head had come back.

"Mio amore, what is wrong?"

"I don't know; this doesn't feel like a normal headache, but I can't figure out what's causing it."

"I will get you some aspirin from the front desk when we get back to the hotel and run you a hot bath. If it does not subside, we will ask Julian about it when he arrives tomorrow morning."

By the time we reached the hotel, the pain had become almost unbearable. Vittorio had already called Chibuike to make sure she would be there when we returned, to help him attempt to figure out what was causing the intense pain.

She placed her hands on either side of my face gently, barely touching, probing my mind. I was scared to let her in, scared of dropping my shields even the tiny bit she required. I was terrified of the blackness, of the First Witch getting inside my head again.

"I believe the First Witch somehow did something to your mind when your shields were down earlier. He is not in your head, but I sense some sort of...stain...a darkness inside you, left behind by his contact."

"Can you make it go away?" I asked.

Chibuike sadly shook her head. "This is beyond even my Power. There is no connecting thread to break as there was with Evelynn. This is more as if he left a piece of himself in your head. Perhaps with Vittorio and Julian's help we might be able to eradicate it, but I'm not sure even the three of us will be able to do anything."

"Shit," I breathed, clutching my head.

Vittorio ran a bath, and I sank into the wonderfully hot water while he held me from behind, sending calming, healing energy to me. I relaxed my shields just enough to be able to receive it, desperate for any relief from the pain in my skull. It only helped a little, and when the water had cooled, Vittorio helped me to bed then called Julian to ask his advice.

Julian called in a prescription for hydrocodone to a local pharmacy, and after ensuring I was comfortable staying alone while he want to get it, Vittorio left to pick it up.

I lay in bed in the fetal position, clutching my head and massaging my temples, tears leaking from my eyes from the pain. I swallowed two pills when Vittorio returned, silently begging Goddess to let it take some of the pain away so I might sleep. It helped a little, and eventually, with Vittorio holding me and continuing to imbue me with soothing energy, I fell asleep.

As I slept, I dreamed of Kevin. This time we stood face to face, as he accused me of murdering him.

"Kevin, don't you remember? It was Elizabeth who killed you, not me," I cried.

"How could I forget the pain of her knife stabbing me through the heart? I know very well who physically killed me, but had it not been for you, they never would have known who I was; I never would have gotten involved in this madness. At the root, it is your fault that I am dead," he said, face calm but eyes lit with rage.

"I'm so sorry," I said between sobs. "I didn't mean it. I didn't know what would happen. I didn't want for you to be involved, and I don't want you to be dead."

"I know, but you are still at fault."

"Can you ever forgive me?" I begged.

He cradled my face in his hands gently. "Of course I forgive you, Elena."

I sighed in relief.

"But you still must pay for what you have done." He plunged his thumbs into my eyes, pressing slowly but firmly, deeper and deeper into my eye sockets.

I grabbed his wrists and tried to pry his hands away from my face, but his inhuman strength left me helpless.

I woke screaming and clutching my head. Vittorio gave me another pill and held me. I drifted in and out of a hydrocodone-induced haze the rest of the night, but never actually slept. I was in too much pain, and too terrified of the nightmares that would be waiting for me.

Julian knocked on the door early the next morning. Vittorio went to let him in, leaving me in bed, still crying from the pain. Vittorio's face was gaunt and paler than usual. Chibuike joined us as well, attempting to help soothe my pain with her Power, but making no headway.

They talked softly, and I didn't bother trying to make out what they were saying. A particularly intense stab of pain shot through my head, and I cried out, "Please, can't you help me? It's getting worse."

"I can try," Julian said, "but would like to work out at Rozanne and Jim's cabin. This is such a powerful force—I can feel it from across the room—that it will be easier to work away from the noise of the city. Do you think you can make the trip?"

"I don't really have a choice, do I?" I said. My T-shirt and pajama pants were soaked with sweat, but I did not bother to shower or even brush my hair, only to put on clean clothes.

I lay across the backseat of Julian's car, half in Vittorio's lap. Chibuike sat in front and guided Julian with directions from the GPS on her phone. I was in too much pain to navigate, and Vittorio was too distracted trying in vain to soothe me. With each mile, the pain grew steadily worse, until the point that I wanted to die to escape it.

"Why would the First Witch try to kill me if he wants to take me as his own?" I asked, hoping conversation might distract me from the pain. It didn't. I winced every time the sun peeked out from behind the clouds.

"I do not know, mio amore," Vittorio said. He thought for a few moments. "Though I have an idea."

"What?" I asked when he hesitated.

"It may be that the First Witch is attempting to pinpoint your exact location, and once he finds you he may offer to stop the pain if you join forces with him. Perhaps he knew you would lower your shields to allow us to help you, and is searching for each of those moments to lead him to you."

"I would rather die than join him," I said.

"I know, mio amore," Vittorio said sadly. "Which is why we must figure out how to get his stain out of your head and defeat him once and for all."

CHAPTER THIRTEEN

I barely noticed when we reached the cabin, and Vittorio had to carry me inside. Julian began removing little jars of herbs from his bag, arranging and mixing, while Chibuike put on a kettle for hot water. I tried to focus on what Julian was doing, but it was no use. At this point, I didn't care if he cracked my skull open and carved out a chunk of my brain to remove the taint of the First Witch; I just wanted the pain to go away.

Chibuike held my hand while Julian and Vittorio quietly talked in the kitchen. I wanted to know what they were saying, and I wanted them to shut up and make me better. The pain was unbearable, and no amount of hydrocodone was helping.

Finally, they came into the tiny bedroom where I lay sweating under a sheet. Julian gave me a mug of hot liquid to drink. I didn't question it and sipped the scalding, bitter liquid. It tasted awful, but anything was bearable compared to the pain in my head. If there was any chance it would help, I was going to take it.

After a few minutes I began to feel floaty. It was a vaguely familiar sensation, and I scratched at the back of my brain, trying to figure out what it reminded me of, wanting anything to help ground me. I finally realized it felt like the times I'd dropped acid when I was in high school.

"What the hell did you do to me?" I demanded. The last thing I wanted was to start hallucinating while the First Witch had any hold on my mind. The thought of what I might see, what I might do, terrified me.

"Relax, Elena, it will not cause you to hallucinate, I promise," Julian said as if reading my mind. "It will give you the sensation you had from LSD, but no hallucinations. I believe this will help ease the pain so that we can more easily work to heal you."

I looked to Vittorio for reassurance, and he nodded while taking my hand. "Julian and I agree that it will be very hard to probe your mind while you are in a state of such pain, nor do we know if it would even be safe. We need you to be more relaxed before we can begin."

"What are you going to do?" I asked, feeling disconnected from my body.

He hesitated, so Julian explained. "I have never heard of anything like this before, so we're not entirely sure how to best handle it. Chibuike told me how she severed Evelynn's connection to you. I know this isn't the same thing, but I think that if Chibuike can lead us to where the stain is in your mind, the three of us together might be strong enough to uproot it and pull it out."

I nodded my head—or I think I did; I couldn't tell for certain with the room spinning so fast. It was a fun sort of spinning though, not like when you're drunk and about to throw up. No, this was like when children spread their arms out and spun around in a circle until they were so dizzy they fell over. The pain in my head had dulled. There was still no way I would be able to stand up or walk or function in daily life in any capacity, but I could hear my own thoughts again, fuzzy as they were.

"How are you feeling, mio amore?"

"The world is spinning," I managed between giggles.

"I think we can begin," Julian said. "Elena, listen to me carefully. I need you to lower your shields. This will not be like the last time; Vittorio, Chibuike, and I will join our shields to protect you. But we must be able to freely enter your mind. Can you do this for me?"

"Uh huh," I mumbled. I tried to focus on my Power, focus on my shield, and to bring it down. I couldn't get a solid grasp on it through the non-hallucinatory haze. "I can't quite get it," I slurred.

"I need you to try harder, Elena. You can do this. We're here to protect you. Now that we know what we're up against, we will not make the same mistake as before, I promise. You know Vittorio wouldn't allow this if he didn't think you'd be safe."

I tried to focus on Vittorio's Power surrounding me. The peridot-green was visible in the air. I wondered if this was why people see psychedelic colors when tripping. Perhaps it was a doorway to accessing unrealized Power. That was an interesting thought I hoped I'd remember later. I shook my head to focus on the task at hand and let my Power intertwine with Vittorio's for a moment. I whispered "Open" softly to myself over and over, willing my shields to let them in. When that didn't work, I physically pictured my shields in my mind—the tall, strong medieval wall. When I had as clear an image of it as I thought I would get, I imagined tearing it down with brute force. I hoped I wouldn't permanently destroy my shields in the process but didn't know how else to get them to lower in this haze.

When my shields dropped, I felt everyone's deep love for me, and their intense worry. And Vittorio's fear of losing me. I felt that he believed it was a very real possibility, and wondered if I really was in that much danger.

Of course I was! The First Witch had tainted my mind. I didn't think there was any greater danger in the world.

Tears formed in my eyes as I felt his fear and pain. I didn't want to leave him. *Please help me*, I begged.

Vittorio wrapped me in his Power, soothing me as Chibuike searched for the First Witch's taint in my mind. I did not feel a jolt like I did when she severed Evelynn's connection, though I did feel her withdraw quickly, almost painfully.

"What happened?" I slurred.

Chibuike looked intently at Vittorio, then Julian, trying to convey something with her eyes to them.

"Just tell me! This is my mind here; I deserve to know. What's wrong?"

"Quite simply, the mark has spread. Rapidly. I do not know if we will be able to remove it, as large as it has grown."

"You have to try! Even if you can only get part of it out! You have to try!" Tears streamed down my face, and I saw Vittorio's eyes sparkle with the tears he tried to hold back.

"We will do what we can," Julian said, though he did not sound confident.

"Perhaps we can try to consolidate it, squeeze it into a lump somehow," Chibuike said. "Then we might be able to wrap it with some of our Power to keep it in check; a binding spell of sorts. It will be a temporary measure, but it might work."

"Do it," I said. "I don't care what it takes, just do it, please." I clenched my jaw against the growing pain. "Fast."

The three shared a look then nodded almost in unison. I felt them enter my mind as one entity. It was as if you had taken three colors of Play-Doh and squished them together, but not mixed them.

They moved in unison, a soothing, warm presence that held the pain at bay. They spread out, the Play-Doh being stretched thin and surrounding my brain. Then I felt pressure as they squished the darkness into a smaller, dense ball. I cried out in pain.

"Don't stop," I distantly heard Julian say. "We're almost there. We just have to bind it now."

I moaned and screamed as the darkness fought them. A violent battle erupted in my skull, threatening to split it open. Vittorio, Julian, and Chibuike were all muttering variations of, "Come on, almost there; we can do this."

Then they started chanting. *I bind si danneggino questa donna.* They repeated this over and over, voices rising and falling, sometimes one fading out as another voice faded back into the incantation.

The dense, black ball they had made of the First Witch's mark pulsed against their Power, trying to expel them from my mind. I didn't think I was going to survive. "I love you, Vittorio," I said, hoping he heard it.

Vittorio's Power surged then, and it was the last push they

needed to confine the ball of darkness–for the time being.

My eyes closed against my will, and I felt nothing.

When I woke, the waning moon shone through the window of the bedroom, providing the only light. For that, I was grateful; my head screamed unlike any hangover I'd ever had. And I'd had some doozies. Warm pressure engulfed my hand, and I knew Vittorio was by my side. I slowly opened my eyes and tried to smile at him, but the smile turned to a cringe from the lingering pain.

"Mio amore," he sighed. "I was afraid I had lost you. How are you?"

"My head hurts, but it's bearable. Aspirin might even work now."

Julian must have heard the request and came in with a glass of water and two pills.

"You did it," I said.

"But at what cost?" Vittorio answered.

"Does it matter? We have some more time now to figure this out."

"I am scared I will lose you before we are able to heal you." A tear fell from both eyes. I reached up and wiped them away, and he held the palm of my hand against his cheek.

"What do we do now?" I asked.

"You need to rest, mio amore." Now he placed his hand on my cheek.

"No way. We don't know how long your binding will hold. We have to figure this out now."

"You need your rest," he argued. "It is vital that you maintain your strength."

"We will talk for fifteen minutes," Julian said. "Then Elena must rest."

Chibuike joined us, sitting cross-legged at the end of the bed. Vittorio sat against the headboard, cradling me in his lap, while Julian took the desk chair.

"I fear the darkness will not be confined for long," Julian said. "I don't know how long we have until it starts growing again."

"What if we haven't fixed this when it does?" I asked.

"We can do this again," Chibuike said. "But the more times we do, the more Power each of us will lose."

"Wait? You'll lose some of your Power? What does that mean?"

"Those who are not as in touch with their Power as we are would not notice a difference, but we all agree we feel as if our Power is just a tiny bit weaker than before. And I do not know if you would survive this again."

"I don't want any of you risking yourselves to save me," I said.

"I would give my life for you," Vittorio said. "I would not be able to live with myself if I lost you, knowing there was something I could have done, even at an expense to myself. I will do everything I can to save you." The fierceness in his voice told me it was pointless to argue.

"I'll call some of my associates in Europe and see what I can find out. Older legends persist across the pond than have made their way here; they might know something to help us," Julian said.

"I'll do the same with the stregas I know in Africa," Chibuike said.

"I will stay with Elena to keep her safe," Vittorio said softly.

I had not wanted to ask him to stay with me, knowing they needed to put all their effort into solving this, but I was relieved he had offered, and wasn't about to argue.

"We will rest here tonight," Vittorio said. Then, after a long pause, "Tomorrow we will go back to the city and Elena and I will try to figure out everything Evelynn and Shane are up to, and how to stop them." He knew me too well to even suggest I sit idle in the hotel room.

"Thank you," I said to him. "Thank you all. You saved me tonight. I owe you my life."

"Just stay alive, and we'll call it even," Chibuike said.

"I think I'll have a little nap now," I mumbled, and laid my head on Vittorio's chest.

CHAPTER FOURTEEN

My head still hurt the next morning, and I suspected the pain would not go away entirely until we had expelled the First Witch from my mind. At least I no longer wanted to jump off a cliff to make the pain stop; this was just an ordinary headache pain. I wore the darkest sunglasses I could find in my bag on the drive back and a ball cap Julian had in his car to help shield my eyes from the retina-burning sun. I took a long, hot shower, and when I was clean I let the water run over me until it cooled. It helped ease my headache a little.

Vittorio and I went to meet Rozanne and Jim at their house then drove to the police station. We agreed to go together to tell them everything that was happening.

It took longer than we expected, as one of the officers wasn't convinced we weren't working with Evelynn and Shane. They all knew the story of how our Power became public, but even my former boss from when I was on the force, Jerry, didn't know the details of what they had put us through the year before. We had to tell the Memphis police some of the details to explain how we knew them to be the bad guys. I let Vittorio take the lead on that part of the conversation.

I was exhausted and ready to drop when we got back to the hotel, but we still had to discuss what Julian and Chibuike had learned that day. I was used to late nights and minuscule amounts of sleep, but the trials I'd already endured through this case had worn me down.

"We don't have anything solid," Julian started. "Legends, rumors, old wives' tales. The sad truth is, the First Witch has been dormant for so long that nobody remembers the truth behind the legends. I did manage to gather a list of herbs that might help prolong the binding, though some of them are extinct, or never existed at all. I have mixed up a tincture with what I have managed to find, and have some of my colleagues sending me others overnight. There is nothing in here that will harm you, though I can't be certain that it will help, either."

"I don't care, just give it to me. I'll try anything."

Once the mixture had steeped for five minutes, Julian handed me the steaming mug.

"It smells like sweaty gym socks," I said. Then I took a sip and pursed my lips. "And it tastes even worse." I forced myself to continue sipping the foul liquid.

After a while, everything got fuzzy as if I had cotton in my ears and was viewing the world through heavy fog. My voice sounded to me as if I was underwater when I spoke, or speaking in slow motion, my words greatly exaggerated. "Fuzzy," I tried to say around my cotton tongue.

"How's your head?" Julian asked.

"Doesn't hurt much," I think I replied, though I wasn't sure if I formed any actual words or not.

"Elena cannot be this unaware and altered," Vittorio said to Julian. "Perhaps it helps the pain, but she is unable to function. She needs to be lucid so she can protect herself if necessary."

"I agree," Julian said, nodding his head. Thick tracers followed as his head bobbed, creating a blur in the air.

Yeah. I was fucked up.

"How long before the effects wear off?" Vittorio asked.

"I can't be sure," Julian said, "but I would think they should wear off by morning."

"Thankshh ffforr tryin'."

"Rest, mio amore. I will stay by your side while you sleep."

The next morning, Julian created a different mixture of herbs for a tea. I hesitated, then drank it. It tasted just as bad as the last one, but after a half hour I felt no similarity to hallucinating. My head still hurt, but it was bearable.

Maybe he'd found the right mix to keep me sane until we were able to defeat the First Witch.

We spent a few days recharging, during which time I had no more occurrences of the darkness breaking free. Julian's tea seemed to work. He scrambled to find more of the ingredients, having to ask a colleague to overnight a few of them to him again. I was drinking a cup every four hours. We didn't really know how often I needed to take it, but I didn't want to take any risks. We experimented with the effectiveness of the tea while it was cool so that I might more easily keep plenty of it with me at all times. The final touch was a healthy dose of sugar to help mask the taste. Now it only tasted like cough syrup instead of sweaty gym socks, though it still smelled just as awful.

All too soon, however, the desperately needed retreat had to end, and we needed to get serious about our problems.

I wished we could have hidden at the cabin forever.

CHAPTER FIFTEEN

Shortly after we got back to the hotel, Mr. Scope called me. I had to hold the phone away from my ear he was shouting so loudly.

"You've made everything worse!" he accused. "My wife and I have been questioned by the police. She took that as a challenge to her 'true family' as she calls that damned coven. She decided she needed to defend them, and went public with her imagined Power. Now the families of the other members of her coven are harassing me day and night. I had to disconnect my landline and change my cell phone number, but they still managed to find my new one. I'm going to the media with my side of the story; I can't keep living like this. I don't even feel safe in my own home anymore."

"I need you to take a deep breath and listen to me for a minute. Please." I heard Mr. Scope taking deep breaths on the other end of the line. After a moment, I said, "Let us take you to the police so they can help keep you safe. If you go to the media, the situation will escalate out of control. We're attempting to avoid a very messy war in which a lot of people will get hurt. Please, I beg you to let us work with the authorities to resolve this as peacefully as possible."

"You've done enough already; how can I trust that you'll fix this? My life is being threatened!"

"Mr. Scope, think about what you're planning to do for a minute. If you go to the media, you will be even more visible. People all over the city, and probably the world, will know what you look like. Is that what you want to happen?"

Silence emanated from the phone. I thought we'd been disconnected when I heard him heave a great sigh. "I suppose you're right. Fine. I'll go to the police and see what they can do to protect me. And I don't need you to escort me." His voice rose in volume. "But I swear to the Christian God, if you don't make this right, I will go public. I will do everything in my power to get witches banned in this country."

I sensed it would do no good to argue with him any further, so I simply thanked him and hung up then told the others what he'd said. "I don't think we have long before he gives up on us. A few days, if we're lucky. I've seen angry husbands whose wives have gone behind their backs for all sorts of reasons, and they are very rarely rational."

My phone rang again. It was a local number I didn't recognize. I answered on speaker.

"Elena, it is so wonderful to hear your voice again. How I have missed tormenting you." Evelynn's voice echoed in the room. "I dared not risk moving any closer to Saint Louis than this for fear you would detect us sooner than I had planned. As it is, Katie's meddling husband has already brought you to town earlier than my plans called for. But not to worry; I will still have my fun with you. I already have, as I'm sure you noticed."

"How did you do that?" I couldn't stop myself from asking.

Evelynn laughed joyously. "Oh, Elena, your Power is so strong, yet you can be so stupid. Did you think I did not sense you lurking in the shadows at my coven's full-moon ceremony? You really must learn to control your shields better. Shane did not know you were there until I told him, but I felt you immediately. I felt your shock when you saw my face, and only then did you become visible to my Power. But it was too late for you; I saw you, and planted that connection so that I would be able to haunt your dreams."

Fuck. I had been careless, and because of that carelessness, had put my own life in very real danger, and those of my friends if it was true that their Power weakened each time they had to rebind the darkness in my mind.

I looked at Vittorio, expecting to see anger at my transgression, but only concern filled his eyes. I asked myself for the umpteenth time what I had done to deserve him.

"Oh, your surprise is delightful!" She sounded like a young girl at a birthday party. "I never dreamed I would have taken you so off guard. I suppose you aren't as clever as you think."

"What do you want, Evelynn?" I said through gritted teeth. I was ashamed and embarrassed at messing up so completely, and I used that to fuel my anger. I knew how to deal with anger.

"I want to see you in person."

"You already have."

She laughed again. "I mean talk to you. See you when you are aware that I see you too. I'll even agree to meet on neutral ground so you can have your false sense of security. Let's make it an early dinner. Four o'clock. The Majestic Grille. Don't be late. And be sure you bring Vittorio. I do miss sharing my bed with him, and think it's long past time he and I had some fun together again." She hung up before I could reply, and I threw my cell phone across the room.

CHAPTER SIXTEEN

The reminder of the time Vittorio had spent in Evelynn's bed, as I was forced to share Shane's, made me wretch. I made a beeline for the bathroom. I wasn't strong enough to deal with her right now. But I had no choice.

"Elena, your Power is buzzing all over the place," Chibuike said when I returned. "The room feels like it's charged with electricity and about to surge at any moment."

I massaged my eyes with the heels of my hands, trying to make the buzzing in my own head stop.

"Mio amore, you must gain control of yourself."

"I'm trying. I need help." I feared if I didn't get control, the blackness would break free of its binding yet again.

Vittorio led me to the couch of the sitting area of our suite. He took my hands and silently helped me ground myself, and regain control over my Power. I took a few minutes to meditate and solidify my control. Then I opened my eyes.

I was a bit calmer but still had a very hard time focusing on just one thought. "Could Evelynn have done something to me over the phone?" I finally thought to ask.

"I would not have thought she was strong enough to do so, but seeing how you are behaving, I am not so sure," Vittorio replied. "I suppose it is possible."

Chibuike sat on a chair across from us. "I don't think it would be safe for me to enter Elena's mind again to search. She is already too fragile. One wrong move on my part could be disastrous."

"I agree," Vittorio said. "We will just have to stay alert and hope that Evelynn has not done anything."

We had no more time to figure things out; we had to leave for the restaurant. I knew I looked awful and hated that I had to encounter Evelynn in such a state. I didn't want her to know how much she'd harmed me.

The Majestic Grille had been transformed from an old theater. The screen still hung, showing old black-and-white movies. Under any other circumstance, I would have been delighted by the decor.

As it was, our dinner companions made my stomach sour.

Evelynn's skin was a few shades darker than I remembered. I narrowed my eyes and refused her offered handshake, as I did with Shane's.

Vittorio was more diplomatic than I and accepted Shane's handshake. He tried to shake Evelynn's hand, but she snaked her arms around his waist, placed one hand on the back of his neck, and stood on tiptoe to kiss him. He gently pushed her away before she succeeded, stone faced and unperturbed. He was a much better actor than I. My fists clenched at my side and it took every last ounce of self-control not to punch her in the face.

"You're lucky I have more respect for the Memphis coven than you do, bitch, or I'd take you out right here."

"No, you wouldn't," she said casually. "You're too good for that." She emphasized "good" as if it were a curse word. "Though I do believe you'll fantasize about it. Just as I know Vittorio will be fantasizing about me tonight while he is between your legs."

"You're wrong!" I nearly spat in her face.

Elena, this is exactly what she wants from you. Please, calm down, mio amore. You know she lies. But if you let her get under your skin, it will be easier for her to manipulate us. Take a deep breath.

I did as Vittorio asked. After a few breaths, I felt more under control. Not completely; I'd never have complete control around Evelynn. She had hurt us too badly, and my rage wouldn't let me. But I was able to say, "If you'd like to think that," and then followed the hostess to our table.

I let Vittorio make small talk while I said nothing. My stomach churned from sharing the same air as those two again, so I only ordered a salad to eat.

"Aren't you hungry, Elena?" Evelynn asked sweetly. "What's wrong? Are you not feeling well?" She almost sounded truly concerned, but then she started laughing.

"I just can't manage to find my appetite with you sitting across the table from me. I feel perfectly fine otherwise."

She studied my face for a few moments. "Why don't I believe you? There is something off about you, but it's not from my mark. Who else is in there?"

I fought to keep my face blank, having no idea she would have been able to sense the First Witch's mark in my mind. Had she become that strong? Or had his mark done that much damage to me that it was obvious to other stregas?

"What are you hiding, Elena?" Shane spoke for the first time since we'd sat down.

I was thankful that the waitress chose that moment to bring our food. I concentrated very hard on my salad until I could calm my mind enough to trust that my face wouldn't give something away. Shock had lit Evelynn's face when she sensed the other presence in my mind; perhaps she wasn't aware that the First Witch had awoken. It was a small blessing if that was the case. I'd rather fight them separately than as allies joined against me.

"Well, as much as I'm enjoying this delightful chitchat," Evelynn said after a few bites of her steak, "let me get right down to it. Elena is getting sloppy. Living in luxury has made her soft. Vittorio, your enchantment with Elena has made you blind. You should have been tracking us more closely. I thought for sure we'd have an extremely difficult time getting here, but you didn't even spare a glance toward us. You made it far too easy for us to create our own coven."

"We made a mistake, and we won't repeat that mistake," I said in clipped words. "Now what do you want?"

"We want you to call the media off. Tell them you were wrong in your conclusion about us. Tell them we are, in fact, legitimate and have caused no one any harm. Let us continue to go about our business as we have been, and we will leave you alone."

"Do you think we'd believe that? That you'd leave us alone while we let you extort money from innocent people and lie to those without Power? Do you actually think we'd agree to that?"

"No, but we thought it would be fun to see your reaction when we asked." Evelynn laughed.

I winced from a sudden stabbing pain in my skull. I looked at Vittorio, trying to convey to him that the darkness was breaking free of its binding. He nodded almost imperceptibly, letting me know he would handle the situation.

Evelynn's face went slack, her eyes vacant. I wondered if she'd had a stroke. Shane frantically tried to wake her up, snap her out of it, anything. He showed far more concern for her than she ever had for him. I wondered absently if he actually loved her.

Then another stab of pain shot through my skull, and once it subsided, Evelynn became alert again.

"What the fuck was that?" I demanded.

Her smile grew. "Change in plans," she said. "If you want to leave this restaurant on your own two feet, and not carried out by Vittorio while you scream through the pain in your skull, you will do exactly as I say."

Shit. She knew about the First Witch. He had somehow spoken to her from my mind, which must be what caused the stabbing pains.

"Yes, he has spoken to me," Evelynn said while Shane looked at her in confusion. "Oh, my dear Shane, you are not so fortunate as to have had the First Witch speak to you as he did to me just now."

Shane's eyes widened. "You're crazy. That's just a legend."

"I may be crazy, but it is not a legend. He has awoken after slumbering for millennia, and we have Elena to thank for that."

My eyes widened.

"You didn't know? You coming into your Power was the

catalyst. The strength of your Power, so wildly uncontrolled in the beginning, was so strong that it awoke the First Witch. When he first made contact with you via the blackness, he knew you were the one he had lost. And now he has found you, though he is not yet familiar with the ways of modern society, so he has asked me to help deliver you to him."

"And what is he going to give you in return?" I asked, hoping my voice didn't shake from fear.

"He will make me his Sacerdotessa. He was going to reserve that honor for you, Elena, but he knows now that you are too stubborn to do as he wishes. He will keep you as his slave. Shane is too weak to be La Guardia, so he will allow Vittorio to fill that role so that he might be tormented every day as the First Witch forces him to watch what he will do to you. Together, he and I will take over the world. We will eradicate all mundanes. We will turn this Earth into a utopia for all stregas who do not defy us. Those who do will wish they hadn't."

"You are insane," Shane said to Evelynn. "Kill all mundanes?"

"Why not? Look how they have treated us. Why shouldn't the world belong to us?"

"You've gone too far, even for me, Evelynn." Shane stood to leave. "If you truly intend to follow through with this, I'll pack my stuff and leave."

"Good riddance," Evelynn said as he walked away. "He'll be one of the first I kill." Her face brightened. "Or maybe I'll force you to kill him, Elena. I know part of you would take pleasure in doing so after what he forced you to do. Oh, I will enjoy watching your conflicting emotions while you slowly butcher him."

I didn't dare open my mind to Vittorio to communicate with him. I looked at him, hoping he would take the lead.

"So what do we do now?" he asked Evelynn.

We followed Evelynn out of the restaurant and got into her car. She would not let us follow her, which in truth, was a smart move on her part. She forced Vittorio to sit in the front with her and rested her hand on his upper thigh. He sat stiffly but did not push her hand away; we were scared of what would happen to me if we did not obey her, at least until we had a better handle on the situation.

Knowing what she had done to him–with him–before made the touch almost innocent. I tried not to let it bother me, reminding myself that far worse things could be in store for us. She drove us back to the house she rented, and only once the garage door was closed did she turn off the engine and unlock the doors. We followed her inside, at a serious disadvantage because I was still scared to open my mind to Vittorio, unsure what Evelynn would do if she was able to gain entry. I felt her probing at my Power, looking for the tiniest chink in my armor, and was thankful I'd at least been able to strengthen my shields enough to fully protect myself during my training with Julian.

She retrieved a bottle of wine from the wine cooler built into the kitchen cabinets, placed it on a tray with three glasses, then led us into the living room where she poured for all of us. She raised her glass. "A toast to new partnerships."

Neither Vittorio nor I returned the toast. It was not something I would ever willingly drink to, and I worried the wine was poisoned, even though she drank from the same bottle as us.

"A toast," she said louder and more firmly this time.

My head started to throb, so I raised my glass but said nothing in return.

Vittorio followed my lead and took a small sip.

"Drink," Evelynn commanded. "It is not poisoned. The First Witch will not allow me to kill you. If I serve him well, he may eventually let me fuck Vittorio while you watch, and then kill him while you are helpless, but he is saving you for himself."

I had no idea how we were going to get out of this, so I took a long drink, praying I would not feel the effects of the strong, aged merlot.

"What do you want from us?" Vittorio asked.

"It is no longer about what I want. Before, I wanted you both

71

dead so that I might be left in peace."

"Did you think we were your only enemies?" I said. "I may hate you, but even I have to admit you are not that stupid. Your search for a coven must have shown you that you have many enemies, or at the very least that you will never be accepted into the community again," I said.

"Of course I know that. But you are the ones who have caused me the most trouble. I have been quite happy with my new coven here in Memphis. I had hoped to lure you down here so that I might get rid of you once and for all. But plans have changed. Now that the First Witch has touched me, I know that I can aspire to much greater things. This council you are trying to form will be powerless to stop me now." She laughed and then winced in pain. "Us. To stop us," she corrected herself.

"You are merely a pawn in his game," Vittorio said. "Do you truly think that the First Witch will let you rule by his side?"

"He has shown me what my life can be!" Evelynn said with the fervor of a newly converted fanatic. "You are simply jealous that I have replaced you," she said to me.

I laughed. "Jealous? I want nothing to do with the First Witch."

"Do not speak with such impertinence in his presence!" Evelynn slammed her fist down on the table, shaking the wine glasses, which were now almost empty. She shook her head as if to clear a fog then filled our glasses almost to the top. "Drink," she said in a soft, shaking voice, then drained her own glass.

Vittorio and I shared a look then slowly sipped our own wine.

"Let's get down to business. I grow tired of your games," she said. "First, you will tell the police that you were mistaken, that while I am asking for donations from my coven, they are for charity. You will say that we have resolved our differences and are now working together so that we might improve strega-mundane relations to show that we are not dangerous."

"That would be a lie," I said.

"Perhaps. But you will do it anyway because you want to protect those you love."

I didn't agree but moved on. "What else do you want?"

"I will become Sacerdotessa of your coven. The First Witch will start his domination there. And you, Vittorio, will rule by my side as my Guardia, and I will again enjoy sharing my bed with you…while Elena watches. Perhaps I will even let her join us once in a while, if she behaves."

I fought to maintain my cool. I wanted to punch her, but I knew that would gain us nothing, however good it might feel in the moment.

"Good. You are learning to control yourself," Evelynn said to me.

She must have seen my internal struggle on my face.

"You are so naive. You see, when the First Witch spoke to me, he created a connection to me from your mind. So I always know what you are thinking now. His Power is vast."

I looked helplessly at Vittorio, unsure how we would get out of this. Perhaps if I did the unthinkable…perhaps if I ended my own life…

No, that would only be a temporary measure. The First Witch knew my soul had returned to the world; he would find me in another life. Somehow I knew it would be easy for him now that he knew what I felt like in this modern age.

We would have to find a way to defeat him–and Evelynn–here and now.

There was no easy escape.

CHAPTER SEVENTEEN

Evelynn drove us back to the hotel sometime after midnight. When I asked why she'd let us leave at all, she said it wasn't her decision. The First Witch wanted me free so he could enjoy my anxiety and suffering while he waited to meet me face to face. It had been a long, difficult meeting, with Vittorio and I stalling as much as possible as we tried to think of ways to get out of the situation. We came up with nothing and ended up telling Evelynn that we would think about her offer. Thankfully, the First Witch seemed to have no problem waiting a few more days, so she agreed.

Julian waited with Chibuike in her room when we returned, worry lining their faces. Chibuike rose and hugged me so tightly that I feared she would crack a rib. I had always admired her openness, her willingness to show emotion so freely. I'd spent my entire life creating a mask for the world so that I might hide my emotions. I did not even let Bryn, my best friend, see me completely; only Vittorio was allowed that privilege. And Kevin, but he was gone now.

We told them what happened. I wanted to stay up and attempt to devise a plan but could barely keep my eyes open. I wondered if it was from fatigue and stress or if the First Witch was playing games with me. Either way, I could not deny myself sleep and was happy the pain in my head had not returned.

I woke late the next morning, and the smell of coffee led me to find the others already awake and eating room service in Chibuike's room. A covered plate waited for me, and I eagerly dug into eggs and bacon and waffles with real maple syrup.

"I fear we must play along for now, until we are able to figure out a solid plan to defeat them," Vittorio was saying. "And we are at a serious disadvantage because of the First Witch's mark in Elena's mind; we do not know how much of what we say he is able to hear."

"This sounds way too much like our last encounter with them," I said. "How does she always get the upper hand on us?"

"We have never had to deal with anyone as devious as she. Evelynn has an entirely different mindset than us. Until we can adapt, we must be cautious."

"He's in my head, ready to immobilize me with pain at any moment. How do we fight that?" I asked.

"I do not know yet, mio amore. Evelynn is even more dangerous now that the First Witch is using her as his pawn. And now that Shane is no longer by her side, we have no idea what he may try to do. The first thing we must do is warn our coven, and tell them everything."

"You know Courtney and Emmett won't stand by idly when they hear about this, even though they have no combative Power."

Vittorio sighed. "I know. They are very loyal. I will try to convince them to stay in Saint Louis and help keep things in order there. That is very important, so perhaps they will agree." He did not sound convinced.

"You are their Sacerdotessa and Sacerdote. They must obey you," Julian said. "You are too kind to them; I understand they are close friends, but you must maintain control of your coven if you are to have any chance of beating Evelynn, much less the First Witch."

"You are right, mio amico. I never wanted to be Sacerdote and have been more lenient than I should. Something to remedy once we are past this battle."

I reached for his hand and tried to soothe him. It had been a long, hard year for all of us, and we were bound to have made some mistakes. Strega or not, we were still human, and no human is perfect.

"I think I should go back to Saint Louis for a few days and organize things there," Vittorio said.

"Let me come with you. I don't want to stay here alone."

"Strange as it may seem, it will be safer for you to stay here, mio amore. Evelynn will see into your mind and know what we are planning, if she has not already. I will speak to our coven alone, and hope that she does not catch on to our plan. And you will not be alone; Julian and Chibuike will stay here with you. I would not leave you if I did not think you would be safe with them."

"Are any of us safe, though?" I asked.

"Unfortunately, no. But I trust them to do their best. Chibuike was once sworn to Evelynn; she will not want to go back to that. And Julian knows how important you are, to me and all stregas, even if others do not see it themselves. As La Guardia of our coven, he is sworn to protect me, and you. To protect all of us. You will be in good hands."

I fought back tears. Even though I'd slept through the night, I was still exhausted, and that was when my depression was most likely to rear its ugly head. I took several deep breaths in an attempt to center myself. It helped only a little.

"All right. I know you're right. I'm just scared," I finally said.

"So am I, mio amore; so am I."

Vittorio called Emmett and asked him to arrange a coven meeting for that night. He did not go into detail on what the meeting was about, afraid that Evelynn might somehow be listening, either through phone taps or through the First Witch's mark in my mind. The mark that now connected her to me.

I found myself wishing I had killed her when I'd had the chance.

"Shit!" I said aloud.

"What's wrong?" Chibuike asked.

I told her the thought that had just crossed my mind. "His hold is getting stronger. That isn't like me to wish something like that.

Maybe in passing, but I've never truly wished I had killed someone."

Chibuike's brow furrowed in thought. "I wonder..."

"What? Do you have an idea? Please tell me."

She took a deep breath. "I wonder if Courtney would be able to help you. She has grown quite capable in her Power of empathy. I wonder if she might be able to take a different approach to containing the darkness in your mind than we have. Perhaps her gentle touch will be more successful than our brute-force binding."

"But we'd be bringing her even closer to danger," I argued.

"That is true, but if we can't figure out how to keep the darkness contained in your mind, it won't matter."

I called Vittorio and put him on speaker so everyone would be included in the discussion. They reluctantly agreed that it was worth a try, so I called Courtney as soon as we hung up and told her what was going on.

"Of course I'll come, Elena," she said without hesitation. "If there's anything I can do to help, I'll do it."

"It could be dangerous for you. though."

"I don't care. I have no combative Power, so there's not much I can ever do to help. I hate feeling useless. This is something I can do, or at least try to do." She paused.

"You don't have to say yes, Courtney."

"It's not that. Could I...could Emmett come with me?"

I sighed. "I know how important it is to have the one you love by your side, but he would be one more person we have to protect if things get out of control. I can't risk that. I hate that I'm even asking you to put yourself in harm's way. And besides, Vittorio needs him in Saint Louis to help keep things calm there."

"I understand," she said sadly then perked up a bit again. "All right, I'll pack a bag and be on my way. I should make it there later tonight."

"Thank you, Courtney; you don't know how much this means to me. And I'm sorry again to have to ask this."

"Don't apologize. You're my Sacerdotessa; I have to do

everything I can to help you. And besides, you've helped me enough. I'm glad to have the chance to do something for you." She hung up before I could change my mind about her coming to Memphis.

I hoped I would be able to introduce Courtney to Bridget while she was here. I had a feeling they would get along quite well and would be good for each other. I knew Courtney didn't have a lot of friends her own age, and sensed Bridget didn't either.

There wasn't much we could do while we waited other than call every strega we knew to see what we could find about the legend of the First Witch. Now that we knew it wasn't just a legend, we could attempt to start sifting fact from fiction. Chibuike was a great help in this, since she had been forced to be one of his wives thousands of years ago when she was barely more than a child. She had been born a thousand years before Jesus, the daughter of a human woman and a god. The First Witch had tried to force her twelve-year-old daughter into his bed before he went off to his war against humans without Power, but her daughter had been stronger than he knew and had sent him into his most recent deep hibernation.

It turned out the soul of her daughter had been reborn in me, and that's why I was the reason he had reawoken. Chibuike knew that before I even trusted her, much less knew it myself, though at the time she didn't know he had awoke.

I shuddered at the memory of my first encounter with the First Witch. I hadn't known then what the terrifying blackness had been, only that it threatened to consume me. As weakened as I was then, I was grateful I hadn't known. I wasn't sure my sanity would have survived it otherwise.

CHAPTER EIGHTEEN

We still weren't able to find much useful information about the First Witch, only that he was purely evil, which we'd already known. No one knew how to defeat him. In theory, he could be killed like any other stregone, and we hoped that his long hibernation had weakened his Power some, but we could not rely on that hope. Chibuike's daughter had drained him of his life force, taking it into herself, which had driven her mad. She ultimately had killed herself, unable to cope with the evil she had absorbed. Vittorio had that Power, but I did not, and I knew that I must be the one to defeat him.

Strangely, that thought didn't terrify me as much as the possibility of losing Vittorio in the fight. It was too frightening of a concept for me to truly grasp. Defeating the first, and oldest, witch in the world, who had been alive for more millennia than humans had written history, or perhaps even language.

I had to focus on what I could understand, so I asked Julian to help me refine my Power. I was sometimes able to mimic the Power of others, which no strega had ever been able to do, so it was difficult to train. And it only seemed to be the more common Powers I could mimic, not rare ones like Vittorio's ability to drain one's life force. It had been a long time since Julian and I had worked on my combative Power; we had mostly been working on healing my mind from my debilitating fear of fire. It had initially been instilled in me during a childhood camping accident during which an ember from a campfire had ignited my sleeping bag. Jonah had the Power to make people feel as if they were being burned alive, which had solidified the fear in my mind. We had made a lot of progress in the previous months, enough that I had even been able to go camping a couple of times with the coven, as well as on a few intimate campouts with just Vittorio and me.

The memory of making love under the stars made me smile. "I have to succeed, Julian," I said. "If for no other reason than for Vittorio."

"I'll help you as much as I can, though we are in the dark. All I can do is help you refine your control, help you concentrate better."

We decided it would be safest to work at the cabin and left Chibuike behind to meet Courtney and drive her to the cabin when she arrived.

Once there, Julian told me I would have to lower my shields a little. Panic set in.

"I can't. He'll find me if I do."

"Elena, it's the only way I will be able to help you. He already knows where you are. Or at the very least, he knows where Evelynn is, and she will be able to lead him to you. She must know about this cabin. It's only a matter of time before they are ready to strike. We don't know where he is right now but must assume he's close. If we operate under any other assumption, it could mean death for us."

"You're not helping," I said, my heart racing and breath coming fast and shallow.

"Concentrate. Focus on your breath. You're stronger than this, Elena. I have felt the strength of your Power, and it is like no other I have encountered. I have seen the strength of your will, and I have met few others–man or woman, strega or mundane–with your determination. If anyone can defeat the First Witch, I have complete faith that it is you."

"All right," I said, letting out a long breath. "I think we should focus on my fear of fire first. He knows that fear and has already used it against me once. I don't trust myself to withstand that yet."

"Very well. Since you say he has already taken advantage of the fear, I need to search your mind to see if he was able to undo any of the work we've already done together. Are you ready to lower your shields enough to let me in?"

The real answer was "Hell no," but I nodded my head, took a few slow, deep breaths to center myself, and lowered my shields the tiniest bit.

"I need a little more than that, Elena," he said gently but firmly.

After a few more breaths, I was ready. I lowered my shields down enough to let him in and was relieved when I felt no sign of the blackness overtaking me. I tried to control my breathing while he searched, tried to stave off the panic that threatened to overwhelm me.

When he was finished, I felt calmer than I had all day. "What did you do?" I asked.

"I implanted a suggestion of calm acceptance. I'm glad it seems to have worked."

"Did you sense any more damage?"

"Miraculously, no. It is possible that, because of who you are, he is not able to do lasting damage to you from a distance. We can use that to our advantage."

"What about the mark he left in my head? I think that qualifies as lasting damage."

"That is something different. That is not damage; it is, as you say, a mark. He left part of himself behind when he first invaded your mind. It is a separate entity from you, and can be removed if only we find the way."

"Julian, since part of him is in me, what will happen to me if I kill him before we get it out?" The panic grew again. Would I defeat the First Witch only to end up dead myself? Or worse?

"I don't know. I've never heard of anything like this, but I hope that tiny part will die. But we can't worry about that now."

"How can I not worry about that?" I shouted, forcing my fear into anger. "How can I risk leaving Vittorio alone?"

"You're losing perspective, Elena. The question you should be asking is, how could you risk leaving all of humanity to fight this force? He amassed an army once, and might have succeeded had Chibuike's daughter–had you–not beaten him then. The world is a bigger place now, with more stregas for him to conquer, more ways for him to connect with those who would help him. He will not hesitate to use even those without Power to help him win the war that will surely come, before killing them all."

"No pressure," I muttered.

"I'm sorry this is how it must be, Elena."

"Me too." I held my head in my hands for a few minutes, gathering my thoughts. "All right, let's do this."

Julian lit several candles. "We're going to start small. I want you to hold your hand close to the flame. You won't actually be able to deflect the flame, so only hold it close enough so that you won't burn yourself, but I want you to get used to the sensation."

I took a deep breath then let it out and did as he instructed. This was easy. One little flame couldn't scare me. I moved my hand back and forth slowly over the candle, bringing it closer each time until I felt the heat. I lowered it to the point of almost burning but pulled away before it did. "Okay, what's next?"

"Very good. I hoped that wouldn't be much of a challenge for you, and am pleased to see it wasn't. Given the limited amount of time we have, I think we should move to a bigger fire. Let's go outside and build a small bonfire."

That alone didn't faze me. I'd been able to handle the campfires on camping trips, though at a distance so as not to feel too much of the flames. I'd even sat around a small bonfire making S'mores with my coven, to no adverse effect. I tried not to think about my childhood accident and followed Julian outside to help him build the fire.

Once it was going strong, he laid out a blanket and instructed me to sit on it, as close to the flames as I could. I sat on the far edge, feeling the heat, inching closer as I felt able. Finally, I made it to the edge of the blanket closest to the fire. It was uncomfortably warm, and sweat formed on my forehead.

"Good. Now stay there and close your eyes," he instructed. "Feel the warmth of the fire. Know that it is a good thing. Fire gives warmth, and life, and good, hot food. Feel that warmth surround you. Accept the heat, and know that it cannot harm you unless you allow it. By allow it, I mean unless you get too close to it, which you will not. I repeat, you are not too close to the fire, and it cannot harm you."

I concentrated on my breathing and felt my heart speed up just a little. I visualized a cool breeze combating the heat of the bonfire. I had never tried that before and found that it worked.

"You're doing very well," I heard Julian say as if from a distance. "Keep feeling the heat surround you. When you're ready, imagine yourself sitting in the middle of the bonfire, unburned. Go slowly; don't try to do too much at once or we may lose all progress."

I continued visualizing the breeze as I also imagined the flames surrounding me. My heartbeat quickened, but I recognized the panic that was about to grow and pictured the breeze blowing my panic away. I was able to imagine myself completely surrounded by the flames, knowing the breeze was Goddess and that she would protect me.

I stood and spread my arms wide as if to embrace the fire. I took a step closer, then another. The smell of the burning wood calmed and beckoned to me.

"Elena, stop!" Julian shouted.

"It's all right; the flames can't hurt me now," I said, eyes still closed, taking yet another step closer. I knew that I would be able to stand in the middle of the bonfire in truth and that I would not be harmed, that I could walk right through it and come out the other side unscathed.

I took another step.

Julian put his arms around my waist and pulled me back. I fought him, knowing I could do this, but he was physically stronger than me and tackled me to the ground, away from the bonfire.

"What are you doing?"

"It won't hurt me. I can master the flames. I pictured a cool breeze deflecting them, and I know I can walk through the flames unharmed."

"Elena, that isn't true. No strega has even been able to walk through fire unharmed. Not even those with Power similar to Jonah's. No one. Do you understand?"

"No one has ever been able to do a lot of the things I can do. Why would this be different?" I was angry with him for interrupting my moment of glory.

"Think about what you're saying, Elena. Listen to your Power. Your shields are down. Is it truly your Power telling you this, or is it the First Witch playing games with you?"

I stopped fighting him, and he let me go. I sat cross-legged in the dirt and searched my Power. "Shit, you're right."

He sat next to me.

"If he's so firmly planted in my head, how can I ever know what is true and what isn't?"

"You must ground your Power more than ever. But you did extremely well. You said you pictured a cool breeze?"

"Yes. I'd never thought to try that before, but it worked. Before I lost control and started walking toward the fire, I pictured myself completely engulfed in the flames, and it worked. I knew I wouldn't be harmed."

"That's amazing! You are very close to conquering your fear entirely. Now I will help you ground yourself so that you will be better able to tell reality from lies. We just might beat the First Witch yet."

CHAPTER NINETEEN

Later that day, Chibuike and Courtney arrived at the cabin. Courtney ran to me and gave me a bear hug. The girl was still somewhat of a mystery to me. She was only twenty years old, and beneath her hard, cybergoth exterior had a childlike innocence to her most of the time, all cheerfulness and sunshine. But she was wise beyond her years and unnervingly perceptive. Part of that was because of her Power of empathy, but part of it was just sheer instinct that few were born with. Sure, she'd been duped by Samuel and Elizabeth, but in the end it brought her to us, and we were able to train her in her Power. For that, I was thankful.

"Are you okay?" she asked me when she finally pulled back from the hug.

"Honestly, not really." Lying to her would only piss her off because she could sense a lie miles away. Not to mention that we'd called her down here in danger's direct path, so the least she deserved was my honesty.

"What can I do to help?" she asked with no hesitation.

I opened my mouth to answer but had no words. I didn't know what she could do.

Chibuike saved me. "I have to admit that I'm really not sure. I've told you what we've already done to try to contain the darkness in Elena's mind. But it hasn't been enough. We wondered if the gentleness of your Power might have a more lasting effect."

"Well, I have no idea what I'm doing, but I'm willing to try if you are," she said to me. "Where do I even begin?"

Chibuike explained how she had probed my mind to find the darkness and suggested that would be a good starting point. "Maybe once you find it, your Power will guide you."

"Are you ready, Elena?" Courtney asked me.

"Ready as I ever will be," I said. I trusted Courtney and knew that she wouldn't harm me; that she was incapable of harming another living being. I did not, however, trust the First Witch and was terrified that if he felt Courtney in my mind he would somehow harm her. "Please be careful, and keep your shields up as much as you're able to against him. I do not want you to get hurt in this."

"I'm a big girl, Elena," she said.

Yes, she was. She had been seduced and used by Samuel, kidnapped by Evelynn and Shane, and none of it had broken her even a little.

Courtney's Power felt cool and refreshing, soothing in my mind. The tension I'd been carrying released. I was almost able to relax. Almost.

I felt her Power jerk back when she found the First Witch's mark in its binding, but she recovered quickly.

"I feel it, but I'm not sure yet what to do," she said distantly.

"Hold your Power there for a few moments," Chibuike instructed. "Perhaps it needs a bit of time to figure out what to do so that it might guide you."

She nodded, eyes closed, hovering quietly in my mind. I felt the moment she realized what she had to do. She wrapped her Power around the binding, as you might wrap a baby in a soft, fluffy towel after a bath; gently and lovingly. *You have been alone for so terribly long,* she said to the blackness. *It does not have to be this way. You can be a part of this world again, part of this community. You do not have to fight this battle. I know our kind is being persecuted right now, but that is the way of humans. They will come around once they better understand us. You do not have to kill them all. Please believe that. It is not too late to turn away from evil.*

She sent what I would almost describe as a tidal wave of love to the darkness, though it was not violent like a tidal wave, but neither was it as calm as the gentle tide at sundown. It was strong yet accepting. And genuine.

How could she send such a powerful, genuine wave of love to such an evil being?

The darkness hesitated, for lack of a better word. It was confused. It did not understand love. It did not understand acceptance. The only thing it understood was absolute power and domination. Courtney's Power was completely foreign to it, and it didn't know what to do with such a sensation.

I felt the blackness pull back into its binding even further, unsure of what to do with this love and acceptance. These were words that no longer existed in its vocabulary, feelings that had been forgotten millennia before even Chibuike was born.

Courtney slowly pulled back from my mind, and I found myself sad when she left. I had felt so peaceful, something I hadn't felt since this whole case started. I wished she could stay there forever, holding me metaphysically. I'd have to ask her if she could teach Vittorio to do what she'd just done. His arms around me would have been the only thing better at that moment.

Vittorio called me late that night after he had met with our coven. He had told them everything, including that the First Witch had awoken from hibernation and was definitely not merely a legend. We had debated that part but knew we owed them the truth, fearing he and Evelynn would attack our coven. They needed to be prepared. Some of the members wanted to leave, but Vittorio convinced them that staying would be safer. Even if they left the coven, Evelynn would know they had once been part of it, and we worried they would still be in danger. Most of the members, however, readily agreed to fight by our sides. Our kindness and justice had served us well. Those without combative Power were also ready to do whatever they could to help.

While Emmett had not liked letting Courtney go to Memphis

without him, he understood the reason. He had always been Vittorio's most loyal friend and agreed to lead all preparations once Vittorio returned to Memphis.

I hoped those preparations wouldn't be needed.

Three days after our initial meeting, Evelynn demanded we meet again. Vittorio had not yet returned to Memphis, so he had to rush to get back in time; she would not hear of delaying it another day.

Julian and I had done everything we could think of to prepare me in the short amount of time we had, though he insisted on coming with us and waiting in the car.

We were fifteen minutes late arriving at her house, and as soon as we walked in the door the darkness started throbbing in my head again.

"He does not like to be kept waiting," Evelynn said.

Vittorio didn't bother to apologize, but I did, promising it wouldn't happen again, hoping it would make the throbbing stop. It dulled but did not go away completely. It seemed Courtney's touch had not done as much good as we'd hoped.

Evelynn led us to the living room, and I failed to keep the shock off my face when I saw Mika sitting in an ornate armchair, waiting for us. She wore a long velvet gown with dragon patterns burned out so that glimpses of her pale skin shone through. She was not wearing a bra. A long slit up the side showed her slender legs crossed gracefully.

"What are you doing here?" I asked.

"My High Priestess needed someone at her side after Shane abandoned her in his weakness and fear. She and the First Witch have promised me the strength and Power to ensure I will never be used, abused, or taken advantage of again."

"I don't understand," I said. "You seem like such a strong woman. Why would that tempt you into joining forces with this evil being?"

"You don't know anything about me!" she shouted. "You don't have the first idea what I've been subjected to in my life. If you knew only a fraction of it, you'd understand why this means so much to me." Rage distorted her face.

"Have you thought about my offer?" Evelynn asked through the awkward silence as Mika stared me down.

"We have, and we do not accept," Vittorio said, as shock at Mika's involvement had rendered me speechless. I had sensed a bit of danger under her friendly demeanor but never would have guessed she would join Evelynn, knowing what she planned.

"Tsk, tsk," she clucked. "That's not a very smart decision on your part, considering whom you will be fighting against."

"We are not divided as we were the last time you tried to take over," Vittorio said, putting his arm around my shoulders.

"That may be so, but Elena is weakened nonetheless. The First Witch has seen to that and can immobilize her on a whim. I'm sure you see that."

Mika rose and sauntered to the couch, sitting on the other side of Vittorio, languidly draping one arm around his shoulder, playing her other hand up and down his arm.

"I do, but that is not reason enough for us to join you. We have been through too much with our coven to simply hand them over to you now. We will fight to the end," I said, sitting perfectly straight in an attempt to appear stronger and more confident.

"Don't you want to protect those you love?" Mika asked in a low, sultry voice. "You could be given Power such as you have never imagined, such that you will never have to worry about the safety of your coven again." She leaned closer, sniffing his neck as a cat might. "You would never have to worry about your beloved's safety again," she spoke into his ear.

"Appealing as that is," Vittorio started, "I would rather protect my loved ones from evil, not send them into the arms of empty promises."

Mika rose quickly, with the grace of a feline, and stalked behind the couch, running her hand over his back and shoulders before she did the same to me, almost carelessly, though I knew each move was precisely calculated.

"Have it your way. That will make it more fun anyhow,"

Evelynn said with a shrug. "He will be arriving in Memphis soon and will enjoy bending you to his will."

"He will never bend either of us to his will," I spat back.

Evelynn just laughed before ushering us to the door.

Mika stood on tiptoe to kiss Vittorio chastely on the cheek before kissing me full on the lips. She winked when she pulled back then walked back into the house with extra sway in her hips.

CHAPTER TWENTY

The throbbing in my head had dulled by the time we got back to the hotel, but the next day it steadily grew worse again. "He's close," I said, sitting on the bed, staring blankly at the floor.

"Are you all right, mio amore?" Vittorio asked, pulling me close to him.

"Not really. The pain is getting worse. The closer he gets, the more my head hurts."

"Could it be that the binding is wearing thin?" Julian asked from the armchair.

"She's right," Chibuike said from the floor, where she sat cross-legged. "I, too, can feel him. I could live ten thousand more years and would never forget the feel of him. It's like sludge, thick and filthy and pure, burning evil." Her brow furrowed ever so slightly, her constant calm cracking. "I don't think he knows I'm here yet; he is probably too focused on Elena, but I fear that he will try to take me as his own again, as he will Elena."

"How on earth can we fight him?" I asked.

"I only know what my daughter did to send him into hibernation millennia ago. I don't know of any other way, though there has to be. All the gods in the myths of old have a weakness. I know those are only myths, but nothing can be truly invincible. We'll just have to do the best we can to protect ourselves until we figure it out."

Now it was Vittorio's turn to stare at the floor. Even though I had my shields up tight, I didn't need my Power to tell me what he was thinking. I looked at Chibuike, and she seemed to know as well.

"You are not the one to defeat him, Vittorio," she said.

"Perhaps if I am able to weaken him enough, though, Elena will be able to finish him."

"No!" I shouted. "It drove Chibuike's daughter mad to the point of suicide. And, if we are to believe her, I am the reincarnation of her soul, the one who is meant to defeat him. What if it kills you?"

"What if he kills *you*?" Vittorio responded.

"There has to be a way for us to get rid of him without any of us dying."

"Elena, I fear we will not all survive," Julian said gently.

I stood. "I won't accept that! I can't! I can't lose anyone else I care about."

"This is about more than just you and Vittorio and your coven. This is about all of humanity. If we don't succeed, at whatever price, the whole world will lose," Chibuike said. "I of all people understand your fear. But we must do what we must."

I sank back to the bed. She was right. Chibuike had lived so long and had lost two daughters to evil witches. Two that she'd told me of. In three thousand years, surely she must have had other lovers, and likely other children. She must have watched them all grow old and die while she was doomed to live forever. I thought about that: to live forever.

"I am not invincible, Elena," she said as if reading my thoughts. "I do not even know if I am immortal. Yes, I have lived a very, very long time. But I know of no other strega like me. I may someday grow old and die. Or maybe I won't. I don't know. But either way, I do know that I can be killed."

She said it with such conviction, and the pain of whatever memory crossed her mind showed on her face, so I did not press for details.

"You're right. Everyone thought the First Witch was a legend. Well, he's not, so it makes sense that the part of the legend about a witch destined to destroy him is also true, and I guess all signs point to me. He sure seems to think it's me, anyway. This is my battle. I will fight it."

"You do not have to fight it alone, mio amore. We will be by your side until the end."

But what would that end be? I didn't ask it aloud, fearing the answer.

"What do you know about Mika?" Vittorio asked.

"Only what I've already told you. She has an affinity with felines, which was made clear by her mannerisms last night. She does not strike me as a person to carelessly get tattoos, so I suspect she may also somehow be aligned with death in some way."

"Death magic is very rare," Julian said.

"Then we must be even more cautious," Vittorio said.

Courtney, who sat quietly in the background through the discussion, suggested calling Rozanne and Jim. "Maybe they'll know more about her Power that could help us."

Rozanne was able to tell us that Mika did have some relationship to death but refused to talk about the details. Mika had said she would tell them everything if she was accepted into the coven, but since she declined the invitation, Rozanne never got any more details.

One more thing for us to worry about. Didn't we have enough to face as it was?

By that evening, the pain in my head had become unbearable. We had to go back to the cabin so I wouldn't disturb the other hotel guests with my cries of pain. None of the pain killers Julian gave me helped the slightest bit, not even morphine. I wouldn't have to worry about fighting the First Witch if this kept up; I couldn't even eat, the pain made me so nauseated, much less stand.

Then the pain stopped.

"He's in Memphis," I said.

"How do you know?" everyone seemed to ask at once.

"The pain stopped, but I can still feel him. He's still in my head, but for some reason he made the pain stop."

I yelped and jumped when my phone rang. It was Evelynn.

"Elena, how is your head?" she asked then laughed. Not bothering to wait for an answer, she continued. "You should come to my home. There's someone here who is eager to meet you."

Calm washed over me. "We'll be there in an hour," I said then hung up before she could respond. Suddenly I knew why the pain had stopped. He wanted a fair battle against me. He was so confident that he would beat me this time because I hadn't been able to kill him before. Arrogance was his weakness.

I took a quick shower and then dressed in jeans and a T-shirt. I walked out to the car, not looking back to see if anyone was following me. I knew they would be, but even if they weren't, I was ready to do what I had to do. I would defeat this monster even if it killed me. I'd already brought enough turmoil to the strega community when the knowledge of our Power became public; I wouldn't let anything else hurt my kind.

CHAPTER TWENTY-ONE

I got in my Mercedes, and Vittorio barely managed to reach the passenger side before I drove off. Julian and Chibuike took the rental car. Courtney stayed at the hotel so she wouldn't be a liability.

"I want her to call Rozanne and go stay with them until this is over." The stoniness of my voice surprised me. I wondered if I was in shock.

"No, mio amore, you are not in shock. You are battle ready. I have fought with other stregas and stregones who could summon a calm determination, but rarely one so complete as yours is now."

I glanced at him from the corner of my eye but dared not completely look away from the road due to the speed at which I was driving. He looked proud.

"You are ready, Elena." He never used my name except in very serious situations. "If anyone can defeat the First Witch, it is you." He rested his hand on my thigh, and I smiled.

I would not enjoy this. I did not know if I would even survive. But I was ready for it.

We reached Evelynn's house in less than forty-five minutes. We had lost the others, but I couldn't wait for them. I marched to the front door, paused a moment, and then knocked. I wanted to burst through the door, Power blazing, but decided against it. For one, they'd probably be expecting me to do something rash like that. Plus, I wanted to get a feel for the First Witch before engaging him in battle as well as attempt to get a better feel for Mika's Power.

Vittorio was right; I was in battle mode. I had never been so calm and rational in my life. Once, I had let my emotions lead me. Then I learned that emotions only get you hurt, so I let nothing more than the sheer determination to live keep me going. My emotions once again took center stage the moment Vittorio entered my life, and he had been helping me find balance ever since.

But this was something else entirely. I wondered if it was how the Berserkers felt before they went to battle.

Somehow, I knew that I could defeat the First Witch and rid the world of him entirely.

Evelynn opened the door with a man I'd never seen before standing to her right, her arm through his. Mika stood to her left, arm snaked around Evelynn's waist.

I tried to hide my shock. He was not what I would have expected. I pictured a large man, maybe seven feet tall, riddled with muscles, black as night. The man at Evelynn's side was my height, five feet seven inches, lean and wiry. His skin was closer to a pale mocha than black, and his dark hair was cropped close. In a simple fistfight I would be able to beat him no problem.

But physical size said nothing of the strength of one's Power. And he had chosen this form to deceive us.

Chosen. Somehow I knew that he could change his appearance at will. He could choose to be the massive man I had imagined if it would serve him in gathering followers. But that was not necessary for us. He knew we would not be put off by physical size. So he hoped to lull us into a false sense of security with this slight frame.

"Elena," he said in a deep, soothing voice. "Elena," he repeated after a moment, testing my name. "It suits you. I approve," he finally said as if it mattered whether or not he approved of my name. "Of course it matters," he said. "For once you are my slave, if I do not enjoy your name, I will give you a better one. But I am pleased that I will not have to do that."

"I will never be your slave," I said emotionlessly.

"This will be enjoyable," he said. "Evelynn, where are your manners? Invite our guests in."

"Forgive me," she said so demurely I thought aliens had taken control of her body. "Please come in and have a drink with us. Perhaps we can resolve our differences peacefully."

I wanted to say, "Fat chance" but knew it would be better to bide our time and play nice for the time being.

"Where are your friends?" Evelynn asked. "Our master is very eager to see his dear Chibuike again."

I should have known Evelynn would have told him she was with us. "She and Julian will be here shortly," I said.

I walked inside, Vittorio behind me, and triple checked that my shields were firmly in place.

We were halfway through our drinks when the others arrived. Chibuike's calm cracked when she saw the First Witch. She refused to look him in the eye and fidgeted while waiting for Evelynn to get her drink. When Mika sat next to her and sniffed the air, she startled before regaining her composure.

"What are you?" Mika asked.

"If you don't know, I don't think I'm going to tell you," Chibuike said.

Mika's lips hovered over Chibuike's neck. Major brownie points to her for not recoiling at the near-touch. "I'll figure it out; don't worry," Mika said before retreating to an armchair.

"So, do you have a name we can call you by? It's a bit cumbersome saying 'the First Witch' all the time," I said, knowing Vittorio would let me take the lead.

"You may call me Akachi."

"Okay then, Akachi. How do I get you to leave me and my coven, and the entire world, alone?" The answer was obviously that we couldn't, but I wanted him to think I was dumb. It was a long shot but worth a try.

"You know very well that is not possible. It would be in your best interest to join me, to willingly be my slave. Perhaps then I will

97

let your coven live."

Mika shifted in her chair almost imperceptibly at the word 'slave.' I thought her eyes narrowed slightly, but it could have been a trick of the light.

"And you know very well I won't do that. I defeated you once; what makes you think I can't defeat you again?"

"You, who are so young in your Power?" He laughed a deep, rich laugh.

It was a good laugh, I thought, then shook the notion out of my head. He was getting to me.

Akachi smiled faintly. "I am already in your mind. You will never be rid of me. If you come of your own accord, I will not make you suffer. Much."

"I would rather die than be your slave." The first hint of emotion cracked through.

He studied me for a moment. "I sense that is true. Then rule by my side instead," he offered.

"What?" Evelynn's hands clenched into fists. "You already have me by your side. You promised me she would be our slave."

"Did you honestly think I would bestow that honor upon you? You have invited mundanes into our world. You have abused our Power. I cannot abide such a betrayal to our kind as that."

"But you said—" she started before he interrupted.

"Yes, I know what I said. I needed you to lead me to Elena. I could have found her on my own, but it would have taken longer, and I am eager to have her back. And now that I have what I needed from you, you are no longer of use to me."

Evelynn stared in wide-eyed disbelief. "You cannot break a vow."

"You are correct, but I did not swear a vow to you. Promises are broken every day. And you were foolish enough to believe mine. And now you will suffer for what you have done."

After a moment, Evelynn realized the gravity of her situation. She stood to run from the room, but Akachi used his Power to throw her against the wall hard enough to leave the imprint of her body in the drywall. Yet she did not fall to the ground; she was somehow held in place against the wall, arms and legs wide as if she were tied spread-eagle, yet nothing other than Akachi's Power was holding her in place.

"Now, Elena, will you stand by my side?" He held his hand out, waiting for me to take it.

I did not move. I simply stared at him, cold and unblinking, letting what I thought of that idea show plainly on my face.

Mika stood and sauntered to Akachi then slid gracefully next to him on the couch where Evelynn had sat only moments before.

He waited a full minute then dropped his hand. "Have it your way. I will enjoy breaking you. By the time I am done with you, you will be begging for me to allow you to be even the lowest of my slaves. And perhaps I will grant you that wish. You will be the slave who performs all of the most difficult, disgusting tasks. And you will be the one that I use most harshly in my bed. Though if you please me, I may allow you the pleasure of being used by all the men who serve me—and the women, if they choose. That will be the highest you can hope to rise for the rest of your miserable life. And I will make it more miserable than you could possibly imagine."

"I would die first."

"I think not. For if you kill yourself, I will make your Vittorio suffer even worse than you. I am inside your mind; I know that you would endure the most horrific of tortures if you thought it would save those you love." He held his hand out again.

In any other situation he would have been right. What he hadn't picked up on, though, was that I was ready to defend all of humanity, even before those I loved.

Once again, I refused to take his hand.

"Very well. Perhaps Mika will be more suited to rule by my side anyway. Her feline wiles have quite captured my attention. What do you say, my dear?" He turned to her, face hovering next to hers as if waiting for a kiss.

Mika placed her hands on his cheeks, moving to meet his kiss, then tightened her grip. "I will never help you make anyone else your slave."

Shock momentarily froze Akachi in place.

"You told me you wanted her by your side willingly, and that you would let her go if she did not choose you. I will never abide slavery!" she shouted before releasing a wave of uncontrolled Power. The room turned icy cold, and I felt the touch of death, the coldness of the graveyard, and what it must feel like to be buried six feet underground trapped in a hard, cold coffin for the rest of eternity, until your body rotted and returned to the earth.

Akachi had underestimated her and was stunned by her attack, eyes wide in shock, and perhaps a bit of pain.

"Run!" she shouted to us as her Power intensified.

I shivered uncontrollably and knew we could stay no longer. We had to get to safety, then regroup. I hoped Mika's attack would give us enough time to escape.

CHAPTER TWENTY-TWO

We escaped to the cars and let Julian and the others get a few moments' head start. I was glad we did because just as I put my Mercedes into drive, Mika ran out the front door. I didn't know if we could trust her, but at the very least I couldn't leave her behind to the mercy of the First Witch. Vittorio got up and leaned the passenger seat forward so she would be able to get in quickly, then I floored it before he even had the door closed all the way.

"What happened?" I asked Mika. "Tell me everything. And make sure it's the truth; I'll know if you lie to me."

"I already told you what I was promised in exchange for helping convince you to join Evelynn and Akachi. But they didn't tell me that if you didn't accept they would force you to join them. I knew Evelynn wasn't a good person, but I never imagined she was that evil. I've been in abusive, controlling relationships worse than you can imagine, and I will have no part of helping force another human being into slavery of any sort. If nothing else, I want to fight the good battle, so I'll help you in any way I can."

I felt the truth of her words and shared a look with Vittorio. He nodded. "All right. We can use all the help we can get. But if you betray us, believe me, you will wish for death. I do not condone violence, but I will protect those I love at all costs," I said.

"I understand," she said solemnly.

"What happened to Akachi?" Vittorio asked.

"Did you kill him?" I couldn't help but add.

Mika laughed harshly. "I'm nowhere near strong enough to kill someone like him. But his arrogance let me stun him enough to allow you to escape. One thing I learned from Rozanne is that my Power is very rare, so he was not expecting an attack such as mine."

"What exactly is your Power?" Vittorio asked.

"I don't like to talk about it," she mumbled.

"If we are going to let you help us, we need to understand who you are, what you can do. I am sorry to force the issue, for I can see it causes you pain, but we must know everything about your Power. Poorly understood death magic can be disastrous," Vittorio said.

Mika heaved a great sigh. "Fine. I told you I have an affinity with felines, which is true. I can also communicate with the dead, and you felt my combative Power."

"How exactly does that work?" Vittorio asked.

"It ties into communicating with the dead. I can somehow call…not death…but the sensation of the grave. People feel like they're dead, or dying, but they're not really."

"Is there anything else?" Vittorio asked when she didn't say any more.

"Well, I don't know what it's really called, but technomancy. I can manipulate technology and bend it to my benefit. I'm pretty good at hacking, and that helps me when I get to something I can't crack." She sighed again. "That's it."

"You seem very troubled by your Power," Vittorio said.

"I hate it!" Mika shouted. "I hate everything about it! I'm different enough as it is; I don't need some crazy magic shit to make me even weirder. A lot of people think it would be cool to be able to communicate with the dead, but it sucks. There's almost always so much pain. I hate using my Power unless I absolutely have to, and even then I wish I didn't have it at all."

"It sounds as if you have been alone with your Power for far too long," Vittorio said. "Perhaps when this is all over we can help you."

"I don't know; no one's ever been able to help me before. And I've always been a loner, more by circumstances than by choice, though lately I've realized it's easier to be alone. That way no one can hurt you."

"If you hate your Power so much, why would you join Evelynn? Even with the promise of never being abused again?" I asked.

"What I said is true. I've been subjected to horrors you can't even imagine."

We let the subject drop and drove the rest of the way back to the cabin in silence while I obsessively checked the rearview mirror every thirty seconds to ensure we weren't being followed.

I nearly jumped out of my skin when my cell phone rang. We hadn't yet reached the cabin but saw the others driving just ahead of us. I didn't recognize the number on the caller ID and let Vittorio answer it on speaker so I could concentrate on driving.

"You will be even more fun to conquer than I expected," Akachi said from the other end of the line. "I did not expect that you would so easily be able to turn your enemies to your side."

"I was never Elena's enemy!" Mika shouted from the backseat. "If I'd known what you really meant to do, I never would have agreed to help you."

"I would like to see you again tomorrow, Elena. I believe that will give you plenty of time to think about my offer."

The pain in my head grew so intense so fast, I had to pull over to the side of the road.

"I suspect you will be ready to talk to me even sooner, but I will make you wait. Return to what is now my home tomorrow night at seven. And feel free to bring as many of your friends as you want; they will be no bother to me."

"Why don't you just kill me now?" I asked through the pain.

"I do not want you dead. I want you as my slave. And it is so much more fun of a game this way. Your fear is palpable, even through the phone. It is quite intoxicating." He hung up before any of us could say anything else.

Without a word, Vittorio got out of the car, walked to the

driver's side, and helped me out then into the passenger seat. He drove the rest of the way, and I was thankful that the pain subsided a little. It was still there, and still made concentrating damn near impossible, but at least it no longer felt like an ice pick was being driven through my skull.

We told the others of the phone call once we reached the cabin. "I think we should ask Rozanne and Jim if their coven can offer any assistance," Julian said.

Rozanne would not ask any of her coven members to put themselves in harm's way. She offered her own assistance alone. "I will not bring Jim, for if this ends how I fear it will, I don't want to leave my coven leaderless. I'll meet you at the cabin tomorrow late morning. In the meantime, I'll take Courtney to stay with Bridget at my Guardia's house. He will be able to protect them."

"I think we should all rest tonight," Julian said. "We can come up with a strategy once Rozanne arrives tomorrow."

No one argued, and even though it was early, we all retired for the night without another word.

Because we didn't know much about Akachi's Power, we weren't able to come up with a solid plan of attack. We didn't even know how to kill him, so the strategy session was useless. We would attempt to stall, talking, so that we might gain a better feel for him, but that was the best we could come up with. No one was happy with it, but we knew we had no choice but to face the First Witch unprepared.

We arrived exactly at seven o'clock, and it seemed as if Akachi had been waiting at the door for us. He opened it with Rozanne's first knock. Ignoring everyone else, he looked directly at me. "Elena, it is so good to see you again. Please, come in. What can I get you to drink?"

"No drinks," I said, my voice monotone. I had entered that calm, battle-ready state of mind again and said a silent thank you to Goddess. I knew I would be terrified otherwise. I tried not to think of the others and focus only on the task at hand.

We again sat in the living room, where Evelynn was laid out on one of the couches. "Is she dead?" I asked.

Akachi chuckled. "Of course not. I would not let her escape so easily. I have seen to it that she will not die until I want her to, though she is unconscious." He stared appraisingly at her for a moment, and I wondered what disgusting plans he had. "Now, have you reconsidered my offer?"

"You know very well I will not willingly submit to you. I'm sure you also know we have come here to kill you," I said.

He nodded once. "Very well then. Your way will be much more painful for you, but if that is what you desire, then who am I to argue?"

The others drew their Power and hurled it at him one after another. He did not fight back, only laughed as the attacks did nothing. I felt the room grow cold and knew that Mika was about to unleash the Power of the grave on him again. I prayed she would be more focused this time.

A great grizzly bear ambled into the room. I had no time to question where it had come from but saw it share a look with Rozanne before attacking Akachi.

With a burst of Power, the bear was sent flying and rendered unconscious. Akachi's neck should have been a ruin of flesh, but there was no sign of attack other than the blood staining his shirt.

Bridget had stood back during the first assault. Now she focused her Power on Akachi, and I saw him struggle to move.

I focused all of my Power, calling upon Goddess and God to give me the strength I needed. I pulled my Power into a tight, dense ball in the center of my chest, and unleashed it upon Akachi.

He slumped over, unmoving. Surely it hadn't been that simple. He couldn't be dead just like that, could he?

I began to summon my Power for a second wave before he recovered when Vittorio shouted my name.

"Elena, watch out!"

I opened my eyes to see Akachi sitting up but had no time to react before he unleashed his Power upon me. He threw me as he had Evelynn, except much harder, so that I broke all the way through the wall and landed on the floor in the den. Somehow I managed to hold onto consciousness, but I was dazed, and unable to move for a few precious moments. Moments in which Akachi was able to attack everyone else.

By the time I was able to stand again, the battle was fully underway. Julian and Vittorio were dazed, Mika was slumped on the floor trying to call a fresh wave of Power to her, and Rozanne was at the bear's side, hands on it, seeming to attempt to heal it. I wanted to yell at her that we didn't have time for sentimentality, but knew I couldn't waste those precious seconds. Chibuike was engaged in the most piercing stare down I had ever seen with Akachi. If looks could kill…I don't know what variety of Power she used, but Akachi stumbled back a few steps.

Bridget again focused her Power on Akachi, attempting to immobilize him, but with less success than her first attack.

I had drawn my Power to me again and attacked while Bridget seemed to use the last of her strength. By that time everyone else had recovered, and we attacked again and again, keeping Akachi unsteady. He seemed to be growing weaker with every barrage. I almost began to believe we might win this war unscathed.

That was when he stood straight, seeming to grow taller, laughed, and attacked me again. This time, I felt nothing, but the world went black.

I couldn't have been out for more than a few seconds, but when I sat up and tried to regain my wits, I saw Vittorio attacking, alone. Still dazed, it took a moment for me to realize what was happening.

Vittorio was draining the First Witch of his life force.

Chibuike's daughter had been the one meant to destroy the First Witch, and even she hadn't been able to endure the ordeal. Something told me Vittorio would not survive the assault long enough to even go mad.

Fate of humanity resting in the balance or not, I couldn't let Vittorio die. I had already nearly lost him twice. I would not survive losing him for good. Humanity be damned, I would save the man I loved.

I pictured every horror I had endured at the hands of my enemies. I pictured the pure hatred I had for the man who had called himself my father. I pictured the pain I felt when I learned of my mother's death, the pain I still felt every day she was not with me.

I thought of Kevin. If we lost this war, his death would be entirely in vain. I thought of Courtney, so young and innocent, with such a dark pain inside her that I had yet to uncover its root. I thought of Emmett and how much he had endured from the public outrage against stregas, so much so that he hadn't even been able to visit his mother on her deathbed for fear that his presence in the hospital would draw the wrath of mindless mobs.

I closed my eyes, holding all of these things close to my heart, and relived my first kiss with Vittorio; the kiss that had awoken my Power. I relived the first time he said, "Ti amo," and the moment I realized I loved him in return.

I bundled all these emotions into a ball of Power, a ball of the purest hatred and the purest love, and hurled it at Akachi with every last ounce of strength I had. The moment I did, I pulled my Smith & Wesson and emptied the barrel into him for good measure.

He fell, bleeding, to the floor.

I called my Power to me for another attack, but nothing answered. Try as I might, I could not feel even the barest thread of magic inside me. I had to pray that the attack had finished him, for I was now defenseless.

I reloaded my revolver and emptied it into him twice more. My ears rang from the shots.

He did not move.

The First Witch was dead. Chibuike had been right; I was the one who was meant to defeat him. But at what cost?

That's when I saw that Vittorio was not breathing.

CHAPTER TWENTY-THREE

For a heartbeat–or an hour–I didn't move. I was rooted to the floor. He couldn't be dead. He had to still be breathing. Maybe not enough for me to see his chest rise and fall, but he had to still be alive.

I fell to my knees then dragged myself to him. When I got closer I would see his chest moving, almost imperceptibly, but he would still be alive.

He was not breathing.

I laid my head on his chest.

His heart did not beat.

I screamed wordlessly then wrapped my arms around him, sobbing into his still chest. He couldn't be dead.

I no longer cared about the rest of humanity. Let them all burn. Every last one of them, even those in my coven. I didn't care. I would make any sacrifice if only Vittorio would take a breath. I would sell my soul to the devil, if he existed. I would trade my own life for his. Anything.

He was not breathing.

"Can't you bring him back again?" someone asked from a distance. It sounded as if I was underwater, hearing someone speak from above the water. It wasn't real.

A small hand touched my shoulder. I jerked then looked up. It was Mika.

"Can't you bring him back?" she asked again.

I shook my head back and forth, back and forth, tears flowing down my cheeks.

"You did it before, didn't you?" she persisted. "Or was that just the media making shit up?"

I looked at her. "My Power is gone," I said almost inaudibly. I couldn't even summon the strength to speak.

Her eyes widened. "How can that be?"

Again, I shook my head, having no answer. I wouldn't have been able to form words to explain it even if I had.

I prayed silently for Goddess to give me my Power back, even if it was just to save Vittorio before she took it away again. She did not respond. Usually I felt a breeze in my mind when Goddess spoke to me. But now there was nothing. Only emptiness and pain. I had thought I would feel good about saving humanity. Instead, I wished for a giant meteor to wipe out the planet. Perhaps that would be display enough of the pain that sliced my heart. At the very least I would be dead and no longer suffering.

Mika knelt above Vittorio's head and placed her hands on either side of his face. Distantly I wondered what she was doing but couldn't summon the breath to ask. Then she placed one hand on my cheek, and I felt the briefest moment of relief. Perhaps she was going to kill me so I would not have to suffer alone the rest of my life.

I was thinking nonsense. None of the thoughts mattered. My soulmate was dead, and I was quite literally powerless to bring him back. I wished I could bring the First Witch back to life just so I could kill him again, more slowly and painfully this time, for taking Vittorio away from me.

Chibuike had warned Vittorio against using that aspect of his Power against the First Witch. But he hadn't listened. And now he was dead. And I was alone. Anger began to seep through my pain. I used that anger, drew it to me like a blanket, pushed the pain away and let the rage burn inside me. If I let pain overtake me now, I feared I would never return.

Mika's hand was still on my cheek. I knocked it away, only to have her put it back.

"I'm trying to help you," she said through gritted teeth.

"What do you think you can do?" I demanded. "Your Power is with death, not life."

"I don't know, but I'll be damned if I don't try to do something. I'm trying to call the touch of death out of his body and into mine so I can dispense it harmlessly. Your anger is not helping."

"How do you know what will help? You don't have the slightest idea what you're doing." I shifted back so I was out of her reach.

"You think you're so great. But you couldn't have done this alone. You couldn't have done it without Vittorio."

"You don't know that," I said. "You don't know us. You can't possibly understand the bond we shared."

"Why? Because I'm young? You should know better than anyone that doesn't mean a thing. And while you wrap yourself in anger, ready to push everyone away, forcing yourself to be alone in your misery yet again, I'm at least trying to do something."

"My Power is gone!" I shouted. "What the fuck do you expect me to do?"

"I don't know, but how do you know it's gone for good? Maybe it will return. Maybe you just used all your reserves and need time for it to rebuild."

"Goddess is no longer talking to me."

"Oh, so that means everything is over?" Mika said, raising her voice. "You're so fucking arrogant, Elena!"

She may as well have punched me in the stomach. Is that what everyone thought of me? My shoulders drooped, and the short-lived anger turned to tears.

"Why don't you do something useful? CPR or something. Maybe if we all work together we can bring him back."

I wanted to believe her. I didn't, but I wanted to. So I tilted Vittorio's head back and started performing CPR, but I was weak. Too weak for it to be effective.

Hands covered mine. "Let me help you," Chibuike said.

Her Power reached into me, searching for the place where mine used to live. Only a gaping hole remained, yet her Power was so strong, I still felt it. I set the rhythm of the CPR and Chibuike provided the force necessary. I took a deep breath, pinched his nose closed, and exhaled into his mouth, filling his lungs with air. Then returned my hands to his chest, rhythmically pumping, willing his heart to beat. Mika kept one hand on Vittorio's cheek, the other on mine, the entire time. I had no idea what she thought she was doing, but I didn't care.

"I'm trying to use your love to draw death out of him," she said.

After two more rounds of this, Chibuike stopped me and said, "Let me try. Perhaps I can breathe some of my Power into him."

I didn't want her to do that. I didn't want her life force in Vittorio. He was mine, not hers.

"Elena, I only want to help. I could never take Vittorio from you. I am trying to give him back to you. Please," she said, pleading with her eyes as well as her words.

"Fine." Somewhere deep down I knew I was being irrational, but I'd just lost the man I loved more than life. How could anyone expect me to be rational?

Julian came to stand behind Mika and placed his hands on her shoulders. Rozanne did the same for me. Perhaps together we could save Vittorio. I almost allowed myself to hope that was true.

I don't know how long we worked like this, long enough for sweat to shine on my and Chibuike's bodies from the effort we put forth. Long enough for my tears to run dry.

Long enough for us to realize that it wasn't going to work.

We sat back, exhausted and defeated.

And then Vittorio coughed.

Vittorio's eyes fluttered open as I cradled his head in my lap. A new wave of tears flowed down my cheeks while I said a silent thank you to Goddess. Even if she was no longer speaking to me, even if she didn't hear me, I had to say it.

And then we heard sirens in the distance.

The neighbors must have heard the gunshots and called the

police. I had no idea how we were going to explain this, and fear washed over me again.

I searched frantically for my cell phone and called Jerry–Sgt. Gerald Lancaster, former boss and tentative friend. "Pick up, pick up, pick up," I begged. After four rings he finally answered. "Jerry, I'm in trouble. I don't have time to explain, but I think I'm going to need your help."

"Elena? What's going on? Where are you?" he asked.

"There's no time. I had to kill another witch in self-defense and the cops are almost here. I'm in Memphis working a case." I gave him the address as the police burst through the door then dropped the phone and put my hands on my head. If they were smart, it wouldn't take them long to figure out I was the one who had done the shooting. The First Witch's blood had splattered me as I relentlessly unloaded my revolver into his body.

Rozanne seemed to have succeeded at healing the bear; at least enough so that it could get out of the house on its own before the police arrived. Small blessings.

"Hands up; nobody move!" the officer in front shouted. Three others followed him, then two of them went to search the house for any other danger. Shouts of "Clear!" echoed through the halls until they returned to the living room, where the carnage lay in vivid crimson. The officer in charge had already radioed for an ambulance and informed the station there was one dead body, and two others barely clinging to life.

The officers handcuffed all of us before loading us in the back of the squad cars and taking us to the station. I begged them to let me go with Vittorio, but of course they wouldn't let me.

"You've caused a lot of turmoil in our city, Ms. Ronen. Yes, I know who you are. Everyone knows who you are now. I don't know what game you think you're playing, but it's over now."

"It was self-defense," I said.

"Maybe it was, maybe it wasn't, but until we have the facts, you're a murder suspect." So much for innocent until proven guilty.

I knew better than to argue and said nothing else. I would wait for Jerry to arrive, no matter how long it took, before I said another word to the police. Even though this was way out of his jurisdiction, I hoped he could do something to help me. At the very least, it would be nice to have an uninvolved friend with me. He may not have understood our Power—correction, their Power. Mine was gone. But he had stopped questioning it.

Whatever happened now, Memphis was safe. Humanity was safe, at least from the First Witch. And Vittorio was alive. Let them lock me up. I could endure anything knowing that he was still alive for me.

CHAPTER TWENTY-FOUR

They put us in separate police cars and caravanned back to the station, where we were put in separate interrogation rooms. One officer was kind enough to bring me a cup of hours-old lukewarm coffee. I didn't care how bad it was. Shock was setting in, and I shivered uncontrollably. Time passed, and the officer returned with another cup of coffee for me. I liked him already, no matter what happened from here. He found me with my legs tucked up on the chair, trying to summon warmth to my body, and returned with a scratchy gray blanket that he draped over my shoulders. I thanked him and asked his name.

"Jeff Richardson," he said.

"Why are you being so kind to me?" I asked. From my time on the force years ago, I knew officers were never kind to murder suspects.

"I don't know who that man is that you killed, but I know who you are, and I know that you're doing your best for our kind."

That made me look him in the eye. He had Power.

"No one on the force knows, so I'd really appreciate it if you don't say anything."

"I swear I won't breathe a word of it to anyone," I promised.

"I'll brew a fresh pot of coffee for you, ma'am, and ask if they'll let me sit in on your interrogation." He rested a hand on my shoulder briefly, and warmth rushed through my body. Then he left.

Soon after, I stopped shivering and realized how weary I was. I folded the blanket, turning it into a makeshift pillow, and laid my head down on the table in front of me. It was terribly uncomfortable, yet I fell asleep immediately.

In my sleep, I dreamed of Kevin. It was the familiar dream of him in a coffin. He opened his eyes, and we were sitting on his couch in our old duplex. A first-person shooter game was paused on his old 32-inch TV, and half-finished beers sat on the battered and stained coffee table he had excavated from his parents' basement. "You did it, Elena," he said, reaching for his beer, and raised it in a toast to me.

"I miss you so much, Kevin. I miss you every day," I cried.

"I miss you too, Elena, but you have to live your life. You can't keep mourning me. Vittorio loves you, and I know he'll take good care of you. You have to let me go."

I jumped when the door to the interrogation room opened. The dream was gone, but I knew I would finally be able to come to terms with Kevin's death.

Officer Richardson followed behind the man who had led the others at Evelynn's house.

"How's Vittorio?" I asked before either of them could say anything.

"Don't worry about that now. I have a few questions to ask you."

"I don't have anything to say to you until Sgt. Gerald Lancaster gets here."

"I don't know who that is, but he won't be able to help you."

I decided not to argue, for he very well might have been right. "Don't I at least get a lawyer? And a phone call?" I wanted to call Emmett and ask him to help find a good lawyer who could help us.

"We have a public defender on the way to meet with you."

"I want my own lawyer," I demanded. I knew there was no way a public defender would be able to save my ass.

"Very well. You may have your phone call then."

This was the second time I'd found myself on this side of an interrogation due to a murder investigation. I'd faced no charges the last time and hoped they'd see it was self-defense this time as well. As the adrenaline wore off, fear crept in. Prison was a hard place, and while I was pretty sure I was tough enough to survive, I didn't want to find out. Who did?

When I reached Emmett, I explained everything and told him I needed a lawyer. He promised to find one, as well as to call Jerry and tell him everything that had happened. I said a silent thanks yet again that Jerry and I had mended our friendship. I didn't think it would ever be as strong as it once had been. He still didn't understand our Power, and his logical mind didn't cope well with things it couldn't explain, but I'd take what I could get. I'd lost too many people in my life already.

I dozed off and on, and when I was awake, tried to reach Vittorio with my mind. Even though my Power was gone, I had to try. The police wouldn't tell me anything about his condition. Each time I asked, I was met with nothing. I prayed that Mika was right about my Power merely being drained and needing time to recharge, but I feared the worst. If I was right, I would lose my coven. I could not be Sacerdotessa with no Power; Vittorio would have to choose someone new for the coven to consider. Assuming he survived, that was.

Both those thoughts made me sick to my stomach.

Shaking my head, I tried to focus on something useful like how to best explain what had happened so I might avoid jail time. The future of my position in the coven hardly mattered if I was behind bars.

I slept again, this time dreaming about Akachi. He spoke to me from beyond and promised that although I had killed him, I would never be free of him. Part of him was still in my mind. He showed me Vittorio lying in a hospital bed, barely hanging on to life. As I watched, the heart monitor flatlined.

I woke screaming, and a female officer I hadn't met yet came to see what the noise was about. "A nightmare, that's all. I'm sorry," I stuttered, shaking from the scene I had been shown. I had no way to tell if it was real or not. "Can I use the restroom, please?"

She didn't say anything and left the room. Surely they'd at least let me relieve myself. Right?

A few minutes later she returned with another officer and roughly pulled me up out of my chair. She led me down the hall to the women's bathroom and went in with me while the male officer waited outside. She then stood outside the stall while I took care of business. Did they think I was that much of a threat? Then again, they didn't know my Power was gone, and trouble did have a way of following me around. I went as quickly as possible, and the female officer stood only inches away from me while I washed my hands.

When I returned to the interrogation room, Jerry sat at the table wearing a visitor's badge. I had never been so grateful to see a friendly face in my life.

"What the hell is going on, Elena?" No small talk from him. It was one of the reasons I liked him so much. That, and he'd been instrumental in saving my life when I was younger and hooked on drugs.

I started from the beginning, from Mr. Scope's visit and me accepting his case, and left out no details. Skepticism showed on his face at the more outlandish parts of the story, such as the apparition leading me to the roof of the hotel where I'd almost jumped to my death, but he listened intently to my entire story. "Please, can you find out how Vittorio is?" I asked when I finished.

"I'll do my best, Elena. If what you say is true, if you killed that man in self-defense, you shouldn't have anything to worry about. But convincing the local cops of your story may be difficult. They've had a lot of unhappy families come forward because of Evelynn's deception. Hate crimes have risen since your press conference. They aren't too fond of you and your kind right now."

"I know, but I didn't know what else to do. If we'd waited for those who had been taken advantage of to tell the story themselves, it would have been much worse."

"You seem to have a talent for getting yourself into compromising positions these days, Elena. You really should be more careful. One of these days I won't be able to save your ass."

"There's one more thing, Jerry."

He raised an eyebrow.

"My Power is gone."

The slightest hint of shock flickered across his face. "How is that possible?"

"I don't know. I didn't know it was possible for any strega to lose her Power. And yet here I am, Powerless, and Goddess won't speak to me."

"Can you prove it?"

"Jerry, you know I can't. Not in a way so that the police will believe me. They'd have to take me at my word, and I don't think they're too eager to do that right now."

"What do you want me to do? Why did you call me down here?"

"I don't know, Jerry. I'm scared. I guess I was hoping since you're a cop you might be able to pull some strings, or at least help convince them to believe me. But I really don't know.

Maybe I just needed a friend."

A small half smile formed on his face at that. "I'll do whatever I can, but it might not be much."

"That's okay. I'm just glad you came."

"Let me see what I can find out about Vittorio. I'll come back once I have something to tell you. Do you know what hospital he's in?"

"They won't tell me anything. I don't even know if he's still alive since I can't reach him with my Power."

After Jerry left, I let the tears I'd been fighting flow.

CHAPTER TWENTY-FIVE

By the time Jerry returned, I had been moved from the interrogation room to a cell. "Did you find out how Vittorio is?" I asked before he could say a word.

"He's alive but unconscious. The official diagnosis is that he suffered a heart attack, but I overhead some of the nurses talking, and they don't really know what happened. His vitals are very weak, but he's holding on. For now." He paused. "I assume you have a lawyer on the way?"

"Yes, Emmett called Vittorio's lawyer, who is familiar with our Power. He'll be here early tomorrow."

He nodded, never a man of many words.

"How are the others? They won't tell me anything about them."

"They're all going to be released soon. The police can't charge them with anything since there's no sign of anyone doing harm to the First Witch other than you."

"Don't they see it was self-defense?" I demanded, slamming my fists on the table.

"I think they do, but they're scared. They don't understand what happened. Unlike Saint Louis, Memphis PD hasn't had any cases involving witches yet. They don't want to take any chances with you."

I sighed, not knowing what else to say. "Thank you, Jerry."

When he left, I lay down on my bed and tried to sleep.

Two days later they released me but ordered me not to leave Memphis. They had tentatively accepted the fact that I'd acted in self-defense and that shock had caused me to fire what they considered an excessive number of rounds into Akachi. I asked them what they had done with his body and was told it was in the morgue awaiting an autopsy.

Chibuike waited for me by the front desk, pacing back and forth, anxiety flowing off her in waves. I could never have imagined her in such a state. "Is Vittorio okay?" I asked.

She stopped pacing and took a deep breath, seeming to just realize what she had been doing. "He's stable but still unconscious."

"Will you take me to him?" I asked, and without waiting for an answer headed for the door, out into the parking lot.

Chibuike followed closely behind but didn't answer. I knew she would take me to the hospital, so I got into her car, buckled me seat belt, and closed my eyes to rest while she drove.

I must have dozed off because when I opened my eyes again, we were at the hotel. "Why aren't we at the hospital? I need to see him!"

"Elena, there are more important things we need to discuss first. I know how badly you want to see Vittorio, but please trust me. I would not make you wait if it wasn't absolutely necessary."

I threw the car door open and marched up to the hotel room. When I knocked on the door, Courtney opened it. I could almost touch the waves of her Power trying to soothe me, even though mine was still absent. I had never stopped to think how our Power must feel to mundanes; this was a new sensation, and something I filed away to contemplate later.

I brushed past Courtney and walked straight to Julian, fists clenched at my side. "What the fuck is going on? Why won't you let me go see Vittorio?"

"We have a very serious problem, Elena. The First Witch has

not left this world."

"What do you mean? I killed him. I put eighteen bullets in him, not to mention whatever I unleashed with my Power–which, by the way, is gone now, in case you haven't heard. So you see, it's not possible that he's still here. I have no way to defend myself."

"Unfortunately, it does seem to be possible. But first, the lesser of the bad news. Evelynn is still alive; she is in the same hospital as Vittorio."

"Why the hell would they put them in the same hospital? Shouldn't they be as far apart as possible?"

"The police do not seem to think so. And in any case, neither of them is conscious yet," Julian said slowly, softly.

"What the hell does this have to do with anything? If she's unconscious, she's not a threat to us right now. Why can't I see Vittorio?"

"I will take you to see him soon, but you must be prepared." He took a deep breath then let it out slowly. "It seems Akachi has found a way to inhabit his body."

I sank to the floor. "What?"

"I believe that when Vittorio was knocked out and you attacked Akachi, he was able to transfer himself into Vittorio."

"What do you mean?" I heard the words Julian was saying, but my mind would not allow me to comprehend them.

"In any other case, I would say his soul, but I'm not sure he truly has a soul anymore. Whatever it is, he is now inside Vittorio's mind."

"But...I don't understand..." It couldn't be true. Julian had to be wrong. "How do you know?"

"I've been visiting Vittorio every day, as much as I'm able between meetings with other covens about the central council. We are making great progress now, given recent events. Yesterday I was at the hospital just as visiting hours were about to end, and very few people were around. I laid my hand on Vittorio's arm to try to reach him with my Power, and the First Witch spoke to me instead."

I covered my mouth as my jaw dropped, and sank farther into the floor.

"Because Vittorio is still unconscious, Akachi cannot do anything other than communicate with people who come in physical contact with him. I strengthened my shields and pulled my hand away before he could do anything more sinister. But as soon as Vittorio wakes…I fear what will happen."

Silent tears flowed freely down my face. After all this, was I still going to lose him? After everything I had endured? Not only had we not defeated the First Witch; we hadn't really accomplished anything. In fact, we were in a worse place than we had been before.

"We'll figure this out, Elena. Somehow, we'll figure it out."

"But if I wasn't able to defeat him with Power, how can I possibly do anything now? How can any of us?"

Chibuike sat down next to me on the floor. "Elena, there's something else."

"What else can there possibly be?" I asked, voice toneless, staring hard at the floor, willing away the emotional breakdown I felt creeping up.

"I think we know how we can defeat Akachi. But you won't like it."

I said nothing.

"I think the only way he was able to get to Vittorio is because his shields were down. He got to you when your shields were down as I severed the connection from Evelynn. I don't believe he can get into anyone's mind if they are protected. And he wouldn't bother possessing a mundane because what would be the point? He wants to kill them all anyway."

I stared at her, not comprehending what she was trying to tell me.

She took my hands in hers. "If Vittorio dies, Akachi will die with him. For good this time."

CHAPTER TWENTY-SIX

I wanted to pretend as if I hadn't heard her. I wanted to pretend as if I was suddenly deaf. But I wasn't deaf, and I had heard her.

"No."

"What do you mean?" Julian asked.

Chibuike was wise enough not to say another word.

"I mean, no," I said louder and more firmly. "Absolutely not. I will not lose him. I can't lose him." My voice broke.

"It may be the only way, Elena," Julian said.

"I don't care. Let the world burn. Let him take Evelynn and kill her instead. I won't let you kill him." I was standing now, fists clenched, ready to fight anyone who got too close.

"Elena, you're not thinking clearly. You've had a very difficult couple of days. We all have. I think we should table this discussion for now and sleep on it. After we take you to see Vittorio, of course. But you cannot touch him under any circumstances. We can't take the risk of Akachi transferring himself to you."

"You said yourself he wouldn't bother with a mundane's body. Aren't I now a mundane?"

"You are something else entirely, Elena. For though your Power seems to have deserted you, he will still view you as someone to conquer. It won't be as fun for him now, but he will take satisfaction in it. He may even take more satisfaction in inhabiting your body than he would simply having you as his slave."

"Then let him take me. And kill me. But I won't lose Vittorio."

"So you would have him survive and lose *you* instead?" Chibuike asked gently.

"He's stronger than I am. Always has been. It will hurt, but he'll survive. I don't think I can survive losing him."

"You are stronger than you give yourself credit for," Courtney said. She'd been so silent, I forgot she was still in the room. Once Julian and the others were released, they thought it would be safe for Courtney to stay with us again.

I stared at her, saw the strength of her belief in me on her face, and decided not to argue. She was still so young. What did she know about losing your soulmate? I couldn't fault her for her naivety.

"Fine. Whatever. Just let me see him." I grabbed my purse and headed for the door. The others followed in silence.

Once at the hospital, Julian led me to Vittorio's room while the others stayed in the waiting area.

I was thankful he had a private room. I didn't want some random stranger to be in the bed next to him. I didn't want anyone to see my pain. And, if what the others said was true, I suppose I didn't want anyone else in the immediate path of danger. Look at that, a part of me still cared about humanity after all. Though I'd still let them all die if it meant I could have Vittorio back.

He lay on the hospital bed, IV in his arm, various wires stuck on his body monitoring his vitals, an oxygen tube in his nose. His chest rose and fell rhythmically. The beeping of the monitor and whir of the machines was the only sound.

Julian hovered at the door, giving me as much space as possible while still being near enough to protect me if necessary. "Remember not to touch him," he said.

I think I nodded, and then I walked step by slow step to the side of the bed. I wanted to throw my body across his, cry into his hospital gown and beg him to come back to me. I wanted to touch him, to reassure myself that he was real, and still alive. Before I knew it, I was reaching out to touch his face.

"Elena," Julian said sharply.

I jerked my hand back to my side and sank into the chair near the bed. Holding my head in my hands, tears falling to the cheap tile floor, I prayed harder than I had ever prayed. I prayed to Goddess, I even prayed to the Christian God of my youth, the one my mother had believed in and tried to convince me to believe in. I'd played along to make her happy but never really bought into it. But if there was anyone out there who might be listening to my pleas, anyone who might be able to save the man I loved, I would pray to them.

Before I realized what I'd done, I rested my forehead against the cold, hard metal rail along the side of Vittorio's bed. As soon as I did, I felt the First Witch. Not in my mind, for I wasn't touching Vittorio, but I felt an evil presence reaching out for me. Filthy desire permeated the air. I felt myself sinking down into a pit as the hospital room seemed to fade to blackness around me.

Julian pulled me back, making me fall out of the chair and stumble. I fell to my knees, and the room reappeared. I tried to wipe the filth from my body, but of course it wasn't real. I'd need more than a shower to cleanse myself of this stain.

That didn't stop me from taking the hottest shower I could stand as soon as we got back to the hotel. I sat under the spray, hugging my knees to my chest, and cried until the water ran cold. Even then I did not move until Courtney came to check on me. She turned the water off and wrapped a towel around me and then helped me stand. She dried me off gently, as my mother had done when I was little, then helped me into my soft, fluffy robe. She guided me to the bed and helped me get under the covers, then sat next to me with her arm around my shoulders.

I wished I'd had the foresight to bring my teddy bear with me.

"I still feel him," I whispered, shivering.

"We may be able to help you with that," Chibuike offered.

"Do whatever you have to; I don't want to feel him ever again."

Chibuike placed her hands on my cheeks and touched her forehead to mine. "I'm going to search to see if I can find any trace of him within you."

I imagined I felt Chibuike moving through my body, but that couldn't have been real. Illusion or not, it was soothing nonetheless. She gently breezed through my mind then down my chest and into my heart then all through the rest of my body. I felt cooler, lighter, where she touched me. When she pulled away from me, I felt more refreshed than I had in longer than I could remember.

I sat up in bed. "What can we do?"

"Elena, you should rest tonight," Julian said. "We can discuss that in the morning when we're all more rested."

"We're talking about the life of the man I love! That cannot wait till morning!" I shouted before remembering we were in a hotel.

Courtney tried to soothe me with her Power, but I waved my arm at her to make her stop. I wanted to feel this anger. Needed to feel it. If I didn't hold onto it like it was my last breath of life, I would not be able to get through this. I couldn't afford to let the fear and uncertainty that welled up deep inside take over.

I lowered my voice. "Julian, please, I don't want to wait till morning."

He sighed then agreed. "All right. I have been thinking about this, and it might be possible to convince Akachi to move into Evelynn's body. If he believes that she is in a better condition than Vittorio, that might be incentive enough."

"But what would that get us in fighting him? Sure, it would save Vittorio, but we'd still have the bigger problem."

Julian gaped at me as if I had just tried to tell him the sky was green. "Well, then we kill Evelynn."

"You weren't joking about killing Vittorio," I breathed. I hadn't allowed myself to truly believe that they would kill my soulmate. Apparently, I had been wrong. "I don't want to kill anyone," I said frantically.

"Are you honestly telling me you wouldn't feel safer if Evelynn was dead, First Witch or not?"

"Well of course I would, but that doesn't mean I'm going to kill her."

"I think it's our only choice." He stared at me, unblinking.

I looked at Chibuike, trying to read her thoughts on her face, but she was carefully blank. That was answer enough for me. She agreed with Julian.

Courtney's brow furrowed as she thought furiously, clearly not knowing which side she stood on.

I had no help in making this terrible decision. Then again, if I was going to agree to purposely end a woman's life, that decision should be mine alone. That was not something to bring anyone else into.

I didn't want to kill Evelynn, and I knew that if we did, it would have to be me who did the act. I didn't want to kill another human being. But how else would we defeat the First Witch? I hadn't been Powerful enough to do so, and neither had the others, so that path was out. I couldn't see any other option besides Julian's. Even if Evelynn never regained consciousness, it would be too dangerous to let Akachi live in her body indefinitely. He would find a way out, and then we'd be back to square one.

"All right," I said.

No one said anything for several minutes.

"Julian's right; there is no other way. But I have to be the one to kill her."

"You don't have to do that, Elena," Chibuike said.

"Yes, I do. I can't put it on anyone else. And while I stopped believing this nonsense about me being something special, I'm still a little superstitious. I don't want to take any chances, and if I am really the one who is supposed to defeat him, then I'd better not mess that up. Again."

I stood, ready to get this over with. "So how do we do this? How do we get Akachi to leave Vittorio for Evelynn?"

"First, we'll have to get them in the same room. That will be extremely difficult. I talked with Rozanne about this. Bridget has the Power of glamour, and she insisted that we let her help us. She is on her way to meet us here now."

"You what? So you were going to do this whether I agreed to it or not?" My heart pounded in anger.

"I'm sorry, Elena, but if you wouldn't see reason, we still had to protect humanity. There is no other choice," Julian said, standing to face me.

I stared him in the eye for several moments then stepped back. He was right.

"Once we manage to get the First Witch into Evelynn, we will inject this into her IV. It's nearly untraceable and is not accounted for in most autopsies." He held up a syringe.

"What if we get caught?" I asked.

"We can't get caught. If we do, we'll all go to jail."

"Maybe Mika could help with the security cameras," I offered.

"What do you mean?" Julian asked.

"She said she can control technology. Maybe she can somehow make it so the cameras won't see us or record us."

"That's a very good idea," Julian agreed. "But are you certain we can trust her?"

"I don't know. I think we can. But if we want to avoid jail, I think we have to."

CHAPTER TWENTY-SEVEN

The next night, we went to the hospital, dressed in nurses' scrubs, and hid in the bathrooms till visiting hours were over. Mika had eagerly agreed to help us, and would draw the security guard away and do whatever it was that she needed to do with the cameras. Luck was on our side that Vittorio and Evelynn were in the same corridor. She was also, technically, in slightly better condition than Vittorio. She was being kept in a coma until she healed a little more so that she would not have to endure the excruciating pain of dozens of broken bones.

We waited for the two night nurses to take a break and then slipped into Evelynn's room. After fiddling with the wires and tubes attached to her, we got her free enough to wheel her down the hall.

I would have to talk to Akachi. This was Julian's breaking point, but I made him see there was no other way. We would place Evelynn's hand on Vittorio's arm, then I would touch his hand for a moment, just enough to catch Akachi's attention. We hoped he would be thrown off guard enough that he would sense the healthier strega body and go to it without thinking.

It was a long shot, and if it didn't work I'd have to resort to my powers of negotiation. I really hoped Plan A worked because my negotiation tactics took more of a sledgehammer approach than anything truly useful.

Taking a deep breath, I sat on a chair next to Vittorio's hospital bed and laid my hand on his for less than a second. The others had joined their Power together to create a shield around me, hoping that would keep Akachi out of my mind. I felt his black stain oozing toward me and felt my friends' bright, clear Power pushing back. The pressure in my head from the battle was tangible, and I clutched it in my hands, willing the First Witch out, and the pain to stop.

In vain, I called to my lost Power, trying to form a shield of my own. I thought back to my very first lesson with Samuel. "What is the strongest barrier you can picture?" As I pictured the tall, medieval stone walls around me, I felt nothing. Goddess had truly forsaken me; perhaps she had seen that I would willingly take the life of another strega. Maybe that was why my Power was gone.

Desperate, I took Evelynn's hand from Vittorio's arm, and held it tightly in mine. With my other hand, I took Vittorio's. If this didn't work, my friends would have to kill me.

You know you won't have the Power you would from Evelynn if you resided in me. You can still make me your slave, and use her as your conduit to the world.

But you will try to escape if I make you my slave, Akachi said in my mind, still mostly in Vittorio. *You will never stop trying to defeat me. If I control you, you won't have a choice but to do as I say.*

You can see in my mind right now. So look! If it would save the man I love, if it would make it so that my friends don't have to kill me—for their sake, not for mine—I will willingly be your slave. Look and see the truth of that! In that moment, I meant it. I forced myself to mean it, to believe it with my whole being. Akachi had to feel the truth of it and move into Evelynn. I would be the conduit, and would have to hope that he did not leave any stain of himself in me again.

The throbbing in my head dulled for a moment. *I see that you do mean this. I also sense that you may later change your mind, but for now, I will take you at your word. You are right: I will enjoy using you for my entertainment, and staring into your eyes as I let my guards use you as well.*

Should you decide to fight me, I will be ready and will make you pay dearly. You will think my previous attentions had been kind compared to the torture I will put you through for trying to defeat me.

He flowed through my body, filling my mind with flames and sending me one last moment of unbearable pain. Try as I might, I couldn't stop myself from crying out. As the last of the First Witch flowed into Evelynn, I fell to my knees.

Bridget and Courtney rushed to the door of Vittorio's room to stop the nurse before he came in. The air thickened slightly as Courtney used her Power to soothe and try to convince him nothing was wrong while Bridget, who was already pretty, made herself appear supermodel-gorgeous and started heavily flirting with the nurse. She said she had gotten lost in the maze of wings and hallways of the hospital, and asked him to show her how to get out. She wrapped one arm around his waist as he led her away, giving us time to get Evelynn back to her room unnoticed.

I hurried to inject the poison into Evelynn's IV, then Courtney and Chibuike rushed her away, back to her own room while Julian helped me back into the chair.

"Can you tell if he left anything behind in you?" he asked me.

I shook my head, staring at the floor. "I don't know. I don't think so, but how can I really tell?"

"Will you let me search?"

I nodded, then he did as Chibuike had done so many times over the past few weeks. He declared me stain-free, though I was too tired to really care one way or the other.

"Can you stand?" he asked.

I pushed myself up out of the chair. I was exhausted, and weak, but I could walk.

"We have to go. Bridget won't be able to keep the nurses away for long."

"I want to stay with Vittorio," I argued.

"You can't. The nurses will have to check on him, and none of us are supposed to be here. We have to go right now."

"I'm staying. What's the worst they can do? Throw me out? Let them."

Courtney and Chibuike returned at the same time we heard the nurses' chatter coming closer. Julian looked at me one last time then said, "Fine, have it your way," and left with the others looking confused.

I was scared what the ordeal had done to Vittorio and wanted to keep watch over him. I didn't trust night nurses who didn't stay at their stations. Surely they'd take pity on a worried girlfriend? They probably didn't get paid enough to bother reporting me anyway. I pulled the chair close to the bed, held Vittorio's hand in mine, and laid my head on his chest.

"What the hell are you doing in here?" A woman's voice woke me up some time later.

"He's my boyfriend. I'm worried about him. I just wanted to see him," I said, willing tears to come to my eyes to help my case. That part wasn't difficult at all. "Please, just let me stay a little longer. I won't bother anything, I promise."

She sighed. "Fine. I'll let you stay fifteen more minutes. But then you have to leave. And don't come back again after visiting hours, okay?"

"Thank you so much," I said.

As far as I could tell, Vittorio had suffered no ill effects from the ordeal. But how could I really know? I would have to be content to leave him in the care of the negligent night nurses; not a very reassuring prospect, but I didn't want to be banned from the hospital entirely.

Sitting on the edge of the bed, I hugged Vittorio tightly, tears falling into his hair, and whispered in his ear, "Please come back to me. I need you; I can't lose you now. I love you more than anything." After kissing him on the lips, I left and thanked the nurse who had let me stay.

CHAPTER TWENTY-EIGHT

When I got to the hospital entrance, Chibuike was waiting for me, sitting quietly on a bench outside. She tilted her head at me, as if to ask what happened, so I told her.

"Wait here; I'll be back in a few minutes," she stood and walked to the door.

"Where are you going?" I asked.

"I need to make sure the nurses won't remember you. If they do, you will be the first suspect when Evelynn dies." She turned from me and continued walking into the hospital.

I hadn't thought about that part. I had been so selfish that I completely neglected to think of that. And if they remembered me, my friends would also be at least persons of interest if not outright suspects. Dammit.

"You're going to have some apologizing to do to Julian when we get back to the hotel. I convinced him that I'd be able to cover your tracks, which is the only reason he didn't go back for you. What you did was very dangerous, Elena, but I know you needed it."

"Thank you, Chibuike," I said and hugged her. "Do you think this will really work?" I asked once we were in the rental car.

"It has to. If it doesn't, I don't know what else we can do to stop Akachi."

"Did you know that was his name?"

"I did but had forgotten it through the years. One wouldn't think one could forget the name of a man who caused so much pain and suffering, but I suppose three thousand years can erase a lot of things." Her voice dropped with wistfulness, and maybe a touch of sadness. What else had she forgotten? Who else?

"I forget nothing important, and pain is never forgotten. It only dims. Yet details often escape me. I may have been blessed with long life, but I was not blessed with endless memory. Most of the time I am thankful for that."

Chibuike's mood darkened in a way I'd only seen glimpses of when she talked about her lost daughters, so I did not press for details.

We drove the rest of the way in somber silence. The clock in the car told me it was nearly four in the morning. I wanted to go back to the hospital as soon as visiting hours officially started, so I'd only be able to get a few hours of sleep. Maybe less, depending on how pissed Julian was at me.

Chibuike must have let him know she was bringing me back to the hotel because he was waiting in my room when we returned. Anger radiated from him.

"Do you know how much danger you put us all in?"

"I'm sorry. I didn't think, and I'm sorry. But I needed to be with him. I needed to see that he would be okay, or at least as okay as is possible given the situation."

"And did you settle your mind?" he asked, not a bit kindly.

"For now." My eyes fell to the floor in shame of not thinking about my friends' safety.

"Chibuike said she has covered your tracks. And Mika used her Power to alter the surveillance tapes so that we will not appear on any of them. I still don't understand those who have the Power to alter technology, but I am thankful we have one on our side."

"Did you tell her what we did?"

"No. I told her it was safer the fewer people who know. Though I have no doubt she'll quickly figure it out."

"How many people have we put in danger?" I asked, sitting down in a chair.

"We must not worry about that. It was absolutely necessary that we do this, and if it puts a few of us in danger, it is worth the exchange for humanity's safety."

"But how will we even know if it worked?" I was terrified of having to face the First Witch again.

"We will just have to hope for the best. If it does not work, I'm sure we'll know soon enough. Now I suggest we all get some sleep. Elena, think about others before you pull a stunt like that again." Without waiting for me to answer, he left to go to his room.

Chibuike slept in my suite that night, and we managed to get about two hours of sleep. She was bright eyed and bushy tailed when we went to get breakfast in the hotel restaurant, while my eyes were barely open. I sipped coffee while picking at my oatmeal loaded with brown sugar and butter. I didn't have much of an appetite.

"Is Bridget all right?" I asked.

"Yes. She waited outside for us, and Julian took her back to Rozanne and Jim's house. She was really happy she was able to help us."

We arrived at the hospital at eight o'clock sharp, and I hurried to Vittorio's room. Nurses rushed about their morning checks, and I didn't bother stopping any of them to ask about his condition. I'd find out soon enough.

A doctor stood at his bedside blocking my view of Vittorio. I stopped dead in my tracks when I heard him whisper, "Mio amore."

He was awake! I ran to the opposite side of the bed from the doctor and threw my arms around his shoulders. He weakly put one arm around me, then the doctor cleared his throat.

"Sorry," I muttered as I pulled away. "It's just that I didn't know he was awake."

"He just woke a short while ago." The doctor continued with whatever he was checking on Vittorio's vitals.

"How is he?" I asked.

"As far as I can tell, he'll make a full recovery. I still don't understand what rendered him unconscious in the first place; he should have woken much sooner after suffering a heart attack. We'll have to run more tests to make sure everything is as it should be."

"When will he be able to leave?" I was desperate to have Vittorio back at my side, holding me at night.

"Mio amore," he chuckled weakly. "Let the doctor do his job. I will be back with you soon enough." He coughed a little and motioned for water.

"Are you okay?" I asked him. I wouldn't be satisfied until someone told me beyond a shadow of a doubt that he would be fine.

"I am tired, but I think all is well. A bit more rest and I will be back to normal."

There were so many things I wanted to ask him, but they would all have to wait until the doctor had left, which seemed to take hours.

Finally, the doctor left, telling Vittorio a nurse would be by with breakfast shortly.

"How do you feel?" I asked.

"Exhausted. And I had the strangest nightmare last night."

"Oh?" I said carefully. I didn't know how much he knew or remembered. "What was it?"

"I dreamed the First Witch somehow had control of me and that you were"–he stifled a sob–"dead. But then I felt your arms around me, and everything was suddenly better."

"What do you remember of the fight?" I hoped the others would come soon. I didn't want to tell the tale alone.

"Not much, honestly. I remember the First Witch throwing you through the wall, and I feared he had killed you. I did the only thing I could think to do, and that was to drain his life force. Everything went black, and I don't remember anything else until I woke up this morning, in the hospital."

"They thought you had a heart attack but couldn't explain why you were unconscious for so long."

"How long was I out?"

"Four days," I said softly.

I was grateful that the others showed up then to relieve me of the responsibility of telling him the terrible truth alone.

"We thought we should give you a little time alone," Courtney said. She looked to be in shock, and I wondered if they had found out that Evelynn was dead. I hated having involved Courtney in this at all. I hated that she had to have any part of someone's deliberate death on her conscience.

Julian looked at me, silently asking if I wanted to tell Vittorio or if he should. I nodded that I would. I wasn't that much of a coward.

"Vittorio, I have to tell you something, and it's not good."

He squeezed my hand, and I told him everything, including killing Evelynn. When I finished, I laid my head on the edge of his bed and cried. He stroked my hair, and I felt his Power trying to soothe me. I tried to answer him with mine, forgetting that my Power was gone.

"Mio amore, what else is wrong? Why can I not feel your Power?"

I sniffed and looked at him, wiping my eyes and nose on my shirtsleeve. "It's gone." I began crying again.

"What do you mean?" he asked.

"I mean my Power is gone, and Goddess won't talk to me anymore."

"Perhaps you are just exhausted. Maybe it needs time to renew."

I shook my head, somehow knowing that wasn't the case. "You're going to have to find a new Sacerdotessa," I said, with a new wave of tears.

"Absolutely not. We will figure this out, mio amore, but for now let us focus on damage control. Our coven loves you. I am certain we will be able to work something out, especially considering why you made this sacrifice."

"But why would Goddess abandon me?" I asked, trying to stop crying.

"No one can know why Goddess does anything. But I cannot believe that is the reason. You have saved the world from a great evil. And do you know yet if she is indeed dead?"

Courtney spoke then. "Yes. I checked her room and it was empty, so I found a nurse doing her rounds and asked what happened. She was really distracted and just said that the patient had died in the night. She barely even seemed to notice me."

"That's probably for the best," Julian said. "The less suspicion we arouse, the better."

A nurse came with a tray of breakfast and told us we should leave Vittorio to rest and eat in peace. I didn't want to leave his side ever again, but the nurse insisted.

CHAPTER TWENTY-NINE

Later that day I was in Vittorio's room. Julian had gone to meet with Rozanne and Jim to talk about the central council. They had made great progress while I'd been busy with the First Witch. Between that and the stunt Evelynn pulled, many covens were ready to listen and come up with ideas on how the council might work. I was disappointed I hadn't been more involved but relieved it looked as if it would be a real thing sooner rather than later.

Because Emmett had been guiding our coven in Vittorio's absence, he went with Julian. Courtney wouldn't hear of not going with him. I think she was spooked by everything that happened, and needed all the comfort she could get. That just left Chibuike, who sat in the waiting room so I could be alone with Vittorio.

During one of Vittorio's many naps, I was startled from the book I was reading to find Shane standing in the doorway. He stared at the bed with a look of horror. "I'm so sorry," he said.

Chibuike appeared behind him, ready to call security if he caused trouble. I shook my head at her, wanting to hear what Shane had to say. The look on his face said that he was not here to stir the pot.

"What do you want?" I asked sharply.

He seemed confused by the question. "I...they called to tell me about Evelynn. I came as soon as I got the message. My phone was off. Do you know what happened?"

Shane looked so lost that I couldn't help but feel pity for him and soften my tone. "I don't really know, but I guess it was complications from the injuries the First Witch gave her."

"Is he...dead?" He looked as if his knees would give out at any minute, so Chibuike helped him to a chair in the room.

"Yes," I said, not wanting him to know that we weren't sure of the answer. I didn't know what his intentions were and didn't want to give him any ammunition.

"Good." He looked at Vittorio again. "I'm so sorry this happened. I knew Evelynn was out of control, but I loved her. I would have done anything for her. So I convinced myself that what she was doing really was in our best interest, forced myself to look away from the crueler aspects of her personality. But once she teamed up with him, once she started talking about wiping out humanity, I couldn't stand by her side anymore. I never thought it would get her killed."

"What are you going to do now?" I asked after a few moments of silence.

"I don't know. I guess I'll go back to my family in Kansas City, see if they'll take me in until I find my feet again."

Pity caused me to say my next words without thinking. "Maybe I could talk to their Sacerdotessa–"

"No," he interrupted me. "Thank you, but no. I know what other stregas think of me. I know they would never truly be able to accept me. I will become a solitary stregone, and you won't have to worry about me causing trouble to the community ever again. I swear it."

I wasn't sure if I could believe him or not, but he looked sincere, so I simply nodded.

He stood and looked at Vittorio one last time. "I'm so sorry," he said and then left without another word.

I immediately called the police to tell them Shane was at the hospital. They'd want to question him about Evelynn, and I doubted they'd like his idea of leaving town.

Chibuike came in and sat in the chair Shane had used only moments before. "Well, that was certainly unexpected," she said after I hung up. "I thought for sure he was going to try to finish Vittorio off, or you."

"I still don't trust him, and I probably never will. What do you think?" I longed for my Power to help me sense the truth.

"I think we can believe him. That's not to say he won't recover and cause trouble in the future, but for now I think we won't have to worry about him."

"Aside from the lawsuit that will surely be brought against him to reclaim the money he and Evelynn extorted."

"He really did love her," Chibuike mused. "I never saw that when I was with the Columbia coven."

Vittorio was released two days later, though he was still very weak and under strict instructions to rest and not worry about any coven business. I would do my best to shield him from the latter but knew it would be nearly impossible. Now that the council was becoming a reality, I knew he would not stand by idly. And we still had to figure out what to do about my place in our coven now that my Power was gone.

"I am going to suggest they allow you to remain Sacerdotessa. Our coven has seen too much turmoil in the past year; I do not think it would be wise to introduce a new Sacerdotessa. And just because your Power seems to be gone, that does not make you any less competent a leader."

"What if they don't want me anymore?"

"Mio amore, have you still not learned that you are loved for who you are, not for your Power or anything else superficial?"

"Aside from Kevin, and now you, I haven't known that kind of love since my mother died, so yes, it is hard for me to believe it."

"And there are many in our coven who love you unconditionally as well. Someday, you will believe that."

"I'm starting to. Old hurts are hard to heal though, and sometimes it's hard to believe that I'm worthy of such an honor."

"And that is exactly why you are worthy, Elena. Beneath your broken pieces, you are humble."

I didn't know how to respond, so I changed the subject. "Rozanne said there's a meeting tomorrow night with many of the country's coven leaders to finalize the central council. They want us to be there. I told her you still needed to rest."

"I can go. This is too important for me to sleep through. If they have made as much progress as they say they have, we must be there."

"Rozanne hasn't told anyone my Power is gone," I said, leaving unspoken the question of whether I should be there or not.

"I am certain there will be some who will not want you involved once we tell them. But your input is invaluable. You must come with me."

CHAPTER THIRTY

Julian went with us to the cabin, for while he was not a coven leader, he had been deeply involved in the discussions while Vittorio and I had been otherwise occupied. Mallory and Alex Bradford, from Kansas City, were the last to arrive, and I was thankful to see friendly faces.

"Welcome, everyone. This meeting will be more a formality, as we have mostly hammered out the initial details. Tonight we will finalize who will reside on the council."

Finalize? They had done a lot of work without us. I didn't know whether to be disappointed or relieved. I decided to go with relieved; I had enough on my plate as it was.

They named leaders from all over the country, some of whom were present, others who had been unable to make the trip. They chose from the larger covens as well as smaller ones that had a lot of activity. Finally, there was only the thirteenth and last member to decide upon.

"Vittorio, we mean no slight to you, but we would like Elena to join the council. We agreed it would not be wise to have both leaders of any coven involved to aid with impartiality."

Vittorio said nothing and waited for me to tell them about my Power.

I swallowed several times, took a sip of wine, and then cleared my throat before finally finding my voice. "I am deeply honored by your offer but am sad to say I must decline."

Small gasps of shock filled the room.

"You see, in fighting the First Witch, it seems as if my Power has left me. I don't understand why, but I have been unable to speak directly to Goddess since that battle. So I do not think it would be proper for me to be a member of the council." I fought back tears as I said this, more upset than I thought I would be.

No one spoke for several long minutes. Finally, Rozanne broke the silence. "Elena has been so involved with the events leading to the creation of this council, as well as introducing the idea in the first place. Vittorio has been almost as instrumental. I propose offering the final position to Vittorio, and including Elena as a consulting member. She will have no say in any of the decisions and will only provide her input for us to consider."

Several heads nodded. A few looked skeptical, but when Jim spoke his agreement, several more followed until everyone in the room agreed to the arrangement.

When the meeting was over, I asked Rozanne if I could stay for a while to pray. She told me to stay as long as I wanted and offered to take Julian back to the hotel so Vittorio and I could have some time alone. I was thankful when he agreed to stay at the cabin while I went out into the woods alone.

I found a clearing, though it was still very dark under the nearly new moon, and sat to meditate. I waited until my mind was clear then prayed to Goddess, asking her how I had displeased her. After what felt like ages, a cool breeze blew through the clearing, yet the leaves did not rustle.

"You have not displeased me in the least, Elena," a voice whispered. I couldn't tell if it was in my head or outside of it, but I knew it was Goddess, and that it didn't matter the source.

"Then why has my Power left me?" I asked, tears streaming down my face.

"You have done what you needed to do; that is all."

"But how will I protect my coven?" It was cruel to have brought me into this world only to tear it all away so soon.

"I think you will find that your coven will not need as much protecting as it has in the past," the voice said. "And should they need protecting, you will find yourself with the tools you need to do so."

I wanted to argue. I wanted to cry and scream at Goddess. But I knew that would do no good. She had spoken to me again; I would have to be content with that, and with the knowledge that the First Witch truly was dead.

After Goddess left, I meditated a while longer on what she had told me before returning to the cabin and telling Vittorio of my experience. "I'm exhausted. How on earth are you still awake?"

"I was worried about you and could not sleep even if I had wanted to, mio amore. I feared what you would find out there. But you seem to be at peace."

"I wouldn't exactly call it peace, but I don't really have a choice but to accept what has happened. Can we sleep here tonight? I'm too tired to drive back to the hotel."

"Of course, but there is one last thing I must tell you. While you were praying, I called an emergency meeting via phone of our coven. I explained the situation to them and informed them of the beginning of the central council and your involvement with it. Every single one of them agreed that you should remain Sacerdotessa."

Speechless, I wrapped my arms around Vittorio and cried into his chest. When I pulled away I realized I'd left makeup stains all over his shirt. My own face must have looked a fright.

After washing my face, we undressed then climbed into bed. As exhausted as we both were, we somehow found the strength to make love. As we did, I could have sworn I felt a whisper of my Power reaching out for Vittorio. "Did you feel that?" I asked.

"I believe I did, mio amore, though it is gone again."

"Maybe there's hope for me yet."

"There will always be hope for you, Elena. Never doubt that."

We fell asleep in each other's arms, and I almost believed that for the first time in a very long time that everything would be all right.

THANK YOU

Thank you so much for taking the time to read *Deceived*. I know your time is valuable, but if you can take a few minutes to leave a review on Amazon I would appreciate that so much. Leaving a review is one of the best things you can do to help me out, aside from telling your friends and family about my work.

And a big thank you to my IndieGoGo backers! I appreciate your support so much, and you were a big part in helping to make this book happen!

Cassie Cathorall
Sean Frazier
Jonathon Green
Kristi Klein
Siri McCarthy
Rosemary Sights
Ella Tiarks
Bridget Walkenbach
Micah Yankowski
Brad Zipprich

You can stay informed at my website, www.JenniferSights.com, where you can also sign up for my email list. I promise never to spam you.